"You've Got No Right!"

"No right?" Lew took two long strides toward her. "I think I have a lot of rights where you are concerned. Even though you walked out on me, you're still my wife."

"You think you've come along in the nick of time, don't you? Saved me from a fate worse than death." Marisa's breath caught in her throat as she looked up into his dark, unfathomable eyes. "In my book, we haven't been married for three years."

"I can never understand ho̶ be such a good actress, Maris̶ cold; but you're not ̶ heart is ra̶

"Get out!"

FAYE WILDM̶ was born just south of London and moved to western Canada in her teens. Since then she has traveled extensively throughout the U.S. and Canada. She describes herself as an avid reader of romantic fiction. Her chief hobbies are music and swimming.

PAPERBACK EXCHANGE
THE WHAT - NOT SHOP
3120 NO. 1 ST. ABILENE
PHONE 673-9221

Dear Reader:

Silhouette Romances is an exciting new publishing venture. We will be presenting the very finest writers of contemporary romantic fiction as well as outstanding new talent in this field. It is our hope that our stories, our heroes and our heroines will give you, the reader, all you want from romantic fiction.

Also, *you* play an important part in our future plans for Silhouette Romances. We welcome any suggestions or comments on our books and I invite you to write to us at the address below.

So, enjoy this book and all the wonderful romances from Silhouette. They're for *you!*

Karen Solem
Editor-in-Chief
Silhouette Books
P.O. Box 769
New York, N.Y. 10019

FAYE WILDMAN
Rain Lady

Silhouette *Romance*

Published by Silhouette Books New York

SILHOUETTE BOOKS, a Simon & Schuster Division of
GULF & WESTERN CORPORATION
1230 Avenue of the Americas, New York, N.Y. 10020

Copyright © 1980 by Faye Wildman
Map copyright © 1980 by Tony Ferrara

Distributed by Pocket Books

All rights reserved, including the right to reproduce
this book or portions thereof in any form whatsoever.
For information address Silhouette Books, 1230
Avenue of the Americas, New York, N.Y. 10020

ISBN: 0-671-57029-3

First Silhouette printing September, 1980

10 9 8 7 6 5 4 3 2 1

All of the characters in this book are fictitious. Any resem-
blance to actual persons, living or dead, is purely coincidental.

SILHOUETTE, SILHOUETTE ROMANCE and colophon are
trademarks of Simon & Schuster.

Printed in the U.S.A.

Rain
Lady

Chapter One

"It's just the thing," John Benton said, a hint of excitement in his voice. "Just the thing."

Marisa Marshall shook her head slowly. Her hands, as they held the bulky script, grew clammy. Who'd have thought that after three years, just to see a name written on the credit of a script could affect her so deeply that she wanted to throw it across the desk at John and scream, "No!"

John sat back in his chair. "Look honey, you've got to do it. Your last film was three years ago. That's fine, and it adds a bit of mystery, but money's money. Frankly, as your accountant as well as your agent, you're broke. Flat, sweetheart."

"And that's putting it mildly." Marisa attempted humor.

"Very mildly," he said. He flicked his hand across his desk and pointed to the script she was holding. "And that's sure money. I mean a Llewellyn Stone screenplay is bound to be a blockbuster."

"Bound to be," she murmured, her blue eyes not showing any of the turmoil she felt inside.

"Look. You can't go on hiding all your life." John was firm. "Marisa, you're too beautiful, too talented. I've turned down too much for you already."

"Maybe I can't act anymore," she said.

"Of course you can. You've got to."

She knew she could. It was instinctive, but not if it meant having to see Llewellyn Stone again. She placed the script back on John's desk and stood up. She was a tall girl. Elegant. Even dressed in casual denim jeans and a pale blue cotton shirt. Her hair, a mass of loose golden curls, clustered around a perfectly featured face. Only a few telltale lines around her eyes and mouth made her look older than her twenty-five years. They unconsciously revealed an inner torment that John, who'd been her closest companion for the past three years, had never guessed.

John stood up and came around his desk with the script and placed it in her unwilling hand.

"Why don't you take it home? I'll call you in the morning to see what you think."

"Sure you're not just in this for your ten percent?" Marisa tried humor again.

"Of course I am and you know it." He grinned. She smiled at his blond good looks, wondering why she could never feel anything but friendship for him, even though he had often hinted at more.

"It would mean a lot to me," John persisted.

She glanced down at the thick wad of paper in her hand. At the neatly typed name—"The Rain Lady" by

Llewellyn Stone. Maybe for John she would read it. Just to please him.

"Okay, I'll take it home," she said slowly. "But I'm not agreeing to anything."

John controlled his delight in having gotten this far with her. "Then why don't you come up and have lunch with me tomorrow? We'll discuss it further."

While she waited for the elevator to arrive, memories of Lew Stone crowded Marisa's mind, but she tried to push them aside. It was hard though, with a chunk of him beneath her arm. Like looking into a mirror and seeing his reflection from behind. Those lean arresting features, the coldness of his gray eyes that could change into a blue hazy warmth when aroused. The black unruly curly hair—the only unruly thing about him.

"Are you waiting for this elevator?" a voice asked, abruptly bringing her back to the present.

"Oh, yes." She scrambled on. "Sorry."

"That's okay," the man said, his glance appraising Marisa's slim blond looks. "What floor?"

"Ground."

Marisa left the building and moved into the late afternoon sunshine where harried workers shuffled their way busily toward buses and subway entrances. The air was hot and stifling. Marisa hitched her canvas bag more firmly on to her shoulder and walked to the street where she'd parked her car. The script was heavy and she held it carefully. It was as though her life had come to a turning point and once she'd read the manuscript, the calm, narrow existence she'd made for herself would explode. Which was silly, she told herself, as she opened the door of her red MG. She'd hinted to John about three months ago that she was ready to work again. And work, any work, meant a change in her way of life. True, Lew had written the script she was about to read, but he'd also written a lot of other things. Yes, it would be her own fault if she allowed herself to be vulnerable again. She had to be strong.

John was right, she thought, as she drove toward her apartment. She needed the work. For her own self-esteem as well as the money. Three years ago she'd been a star. Beautiful, successful. And now? Now, she had recovered from the breakup with Lew, from a near nervous breakdown, from all that had turned delirious happiness into a raging nightmare.

When Marisa arrived at the apartment building she lived in, she parked her car in the underground garage and emptied her mailbox before getting into the elevator that would take her to the tenth floor. Glancing through the mail, she saw that, as usual, most of the letters were bills or advertising. Not one of her former friends knew where she was. She'd succeeded in cutting herself off from the world. Even the media had finally given up searching and gone on to greener pastures. Tomorrow she would hand the bills to John who would pay them as he'd done for the past three years. Poor John. When he'd signed on as her agent, he'd thought he had a ready-made star. He had not reckoned on her premature retirement.

Marisa let herself into the apartment, disposed of her mail and the script on a small side table, and then walked through to the living room. She loved this room with its soft, tan leather chairs and sofa, its thick, cream rug and natural wood tables. The bedroom was almost a continuation of the living room—the cream rug and a large bed covered with a brightly colored spread and cushions. It was a sealed and air-conditioned existence out of which she sometimes had the claustrophobic urge to flee, while at other times she was glad for her comfortable hiding place.

She looked out the large window in the living room to other high-rise apartment buildings and the green of trees, to where bridges and a network of busy highways cut through the undulating hills of the Don Valley. Then, in the distance, the city of Toronto. The sun was glinting on the windows of the buildings.

Marisa turned away and ran agitated fingers through her golden curls. The full implication of having the script had hit her. Of course, it meant that Lew now knew where she was. Well, sooner or later he would have found her. She sighed and went and filled a pot of coffee to put on the stove to perk. Then she got out some eggs to make an omelette. Lew's manuscript sat on her table and waited for her to begin reading.

It was past midnight when Marisa finally put down the script. Scraps of her hasty meal stood beside the empty coffee pot on the table. She'd always known Lew was a good writer, but she'd never credited him with anything as powerful as the manuscript she'd just read.

She released a breath in a sigh and tried to rid herself of the trembling emotion the story had caused. It was excellent. It would be a great film. Something an actress could really get her teeth into. Already just by reading it, she felt akin to the heroine, Marion Darnell, who wrought an innocent destruction throughout her short life.

Not that Marisa had any reason to believe that her life could in any way parallel the dramatization. Marion Darnell, a rather pathetic creature, discovered the deception of her fiancé, Roland, and retaliated by becoming promiscuous and causing others hurt as Roland had hurt her. In the end she reconciled with Roland, and, as Roland's new bride, when the true thoughtlessness of her actions came to her, she committed suicide.

Marisa got up and walked across to the window. The panoramic view was changed now by darkness. Winking neon lights beckoned her to go out and join in the excitement, have her name flash once again on a cinema marquee. The pull was almost physical. She should do the film. It would be a brilliant comeback if she could muster the strength to act the part. It had to have the right producer, the right director. Not just big money out to make a killing, but someone who cared. John hadn't mentioned the film company or told her anything about the director, producer, other actors, or where it was to be filmed. She'd ask him all that at lunch tomorrow. Or today. She looked ruefully across at the luminous dial of her wall clock. Maybe she could make the film and not even have to meet Llewellyn Stone again.

"Are you saying you'll do it?" John looked happy but surprised when Marisa told him of her decision the next morning in his office.

"I'll have an audition," Marisa told him. "It's a powerful script."

"The best of Llewellyn Stone, believe me," John said. "And don't worry. You're spoken for."

"Spoken for?" Marisa repeated. "By whom?"

"Stone films," John told her.

"I see," she said.

"What do you see?" John asked.

"Stone films is Lew Stone isn't it?"

"Of course," John said with a shrug of his shoulders.

Marisa took a deep breath. "I told you I wanted no one to know where I was."

"But I don't understand." John looked puzzled. "You mentioned a while back that you wanted to work. I started hunting around and Lew Stone approached me. I know it's the big time, but why not start back with a rush?"

Marisa's lips trembled. John didn't know about her relationship with Lew Stone. It had been one of the best kept secrets ever.

"Look, honey," John sighed. "Lew Stone wants to come home and make this film in Toronto. It's a good place to make films these days and it's almost as though the part were written for you."

Marisa turned away. She got up and paced the office floor restlessly. John stood up and rustled some papers on his desk.

"I'm beginning to have my suspicions that it's Lew Stone you're scared of, not the acting," he said.

Marisa still didn't face him.

"I've met him," John went on. "He's a nice guy. Matter-of-fact, down-to-business type. He'll make a great job of this film. That other thing he did, 'Melodrama,' I went to see it four times. It was really great."

"Good for you," Marisa muttered.

"So it is Stone. What did he do to you?"

She couldn't explain all the agony and hurt in a few short sentences. She composed herself and turned around to face John. He was standing, staring at her, a puzzled look on his handsome face.

"I knew him once," she said lightly. "I just don't care for him, that's all."

"Is that a good reason for turning down the chance of a lifetime?" John asked.

She shook her head. John came around his desk to stand beside her. "I don't want you hurt Marisa. But, it's a chance to get back to the glitter. You still have fan clubs around the world. You're still known."

"I don't think so," she murmured.

"Then you only have yourself to blame for it," John said curtly.

"And Lew," she told herself silently.

John's expression turned hard. "Okay. What if I tell you that you're more than just broke? That you're in debt, to me personally, as well as to the bank and other creditors? What if I told you that?"

She sighed tremulously.

"Well?" he demanded.

"You're blackmailing me."

"No I'm not. It really *is* that bad, and I don't want to go out of business. I still have Clara and the kids to support and this is a chance for both of us to make a buck. It's not worth ruining the chance just because you and Lew Stone rub each other the wrong way."

Marisa's blue eyes were haunted. "I think it's a great script, John. I really do. I'd like to do it for you, but . . ."

"But what?" John was angry. "You won't have to see the man other than professionally. Just keep it cool. I know you can handle it, Marisa. You're a great actress."

"Not that great," she muttered.

"Don't be so unreasonable." John had clearly lost his patience with her. "I thought the man was honest and straightforward. I liked him."

"You don't understand, John," she pleaded, wondering if she should pour out the whole story. Not even three years had dulled the raw hurt she felt by remembering.

"I do understand," he told her, "but understanding doesn't feed the bank balance. I have a contract for you that's excellent." He picked up a brown envelope stuffed with papers. "And I want you to sign it."

"I'm not signing anything," Marisa said stubbornly.

John sighed. "Whatever you might think about the man, his business acumen is right on. This is a good contract."

"Anyone but Lew Stone," she told him, "just anyone but him."

"But he wants you," John told her, replacing the envelope with the contract on his desk. He looked dejected. "I know I can't force you to do anything, but I had hoped that you would want to help me."

"I do. John, really I do," she pleaded.

"Then do this for me. Please?"

"Can I have another night to think it over?" she asked, grasping for time.

He looked at her for a moment, then shrugged. "Okay," he said. "Why not?" He smiled faintly. "Come on, let's go and have some lunch and blow the budget completely."

Chapter Two

John didn't persist or push her about the script. Their conversation at lunch was far removed from the film world. John told her about his latest visit with his two children. Once in a while Marisa would accompany John and the children, a ten-year-old boy and four-year-old girl, on their trips to the cinema or the zoo, but she had always felt slightly apart from the little family group, knowing that she could never be what John wanted her to be—his wife.

After lunch John had to get back to the office and Marisa, promising her decision the next day, stayed in the city to shop before returning home. As she restlessly moved through crowded streets and stores, she remembered back to a time when she couldn't walk around and not be noticed, a time when she'd adorned the pages of every magazine and entertainment page in North America and Europe. '

Born in a small, southern Ontario town, Marisa's childhood had been lonely and unhappy. Her parents had been stern and cold. Both had died in a car crash when she was barely eight. She had been shunted to her mother's spinster sister, who had been even stricter than her parents. When her aunt had died from a heart attack shortly before Marisa's seventeenth birthday, Marisa had felt more relief than grief. She could not help rejoicing in her first taste of freedom. She did what she'd always dreamed of doing. She took her small inheritance and traveled to California. She was going to fulfill her lifelong dream of being an actress.

Acting had been easy for her, probably because as a child she'd been alone so much that she had had to invent all her play situations. But it hadn't been so easy getting work. Hollywood was swamped with girls like herself. To eat and pay her rent she had had to take part-time work in the local library, while still continuing with her acting lessons.

She had met Llewellyn Stone at the library on a particularly busy morning. She was placing a couple of books on a high shelf when she felt that someone was watching her. Self-consciously, she pulled at the brief pink top she was wearing so that it didn't show quite so much of her tanned middle. In doing so she dropped the books.

"Damn," she muttered to herself, and turned around to find that the man who had been watching her, had picked up the books. He handed them to her, amusement in his gray eyes.

"You shouldn't try to do two things at once," he told her.

"I wasn't, I—" Marisa said, and then smiled. "You shouldn't stare."

"Then you shouldn't look so delectable," he grinned. "Do you work here often?"

"Three days a week," she told him, trying to determine if he were a movie star. He certainly had the looks. He was deeply tanned, with lean features and a smile that was startlingly white. His hair was an unruly mass of dark curls. He was wearing a black leather bomber jacket and a navy turtleneck sweater. Slim fitting blue cords hugged his body closely.

"Trying to place me?" he asked, interrupting her thoughts.

"I—I just wondered—"

"Llewellyn Stone," he said, "scriptwriter."

"Glad to meet you Mr. Stone." Her hand met to shake his tanned fingers in mid-air.

"Glad to meet you—?" His dark eyebrows rose in question.

"Marisa," she told him, "Marisa Marshall."

"Actress?" he asked.

"Not yet," she told him, breathlessly, "but hoping."

His eyes raked her slim body in its deep pink slacks and lighter pink top. He took in the lovely, blond hair.

"I'd stick to libraries if I were you," he told her briskly. "Would you like to do some work for me?"

"I'd be delighted," she told him.

The work had turned out to be research for one of his scripts and Marisa came to see Lew Stone as often as he visited the library, summoned by one of her phone calls to tell him that she'd found the information he needed.

Thursday was her evening to work late. Lew Stone

had arrived about two hours ago and they were sitting across a table while she pointed out some of the information she had gathered for him. She relayed, rather self-consciously, some of her own ideas on the subject.

He smiled at her while writing something in the margin of a sheet.

"You're doing well," he said. "Sure you wouldn't like to get into this side of film rather than acting?"

"I want to act," she told him. "That's all I really want to do."

"Then we'll have to see what we can do," he said, packing up his work.

"You mean you're going to help me?" Marisa's blue eyes shone.

"Maybe," he told her. "I'll see what I can do."

"If you could," she said eagerly, "if you could—"

"If I could what?" He eyed her with amusement.

"I—I'd be indebted to you I suppose," she said quietly.

"I suppose you would." He slipped his papers into the slim leather briefcase he always brought with him. "Can I see you home?"

It was nine o'clock, and time she left, so she accepted his offer and was soon in his Jaguar giving him directions toward her apartment.

"I'm going to New York tomorrow," he said, after a while.

"What are you going to do there?" she asked.

"Bargain over this script," he told her.

"But you haven't written it yet."

"The idea is there. I have to get it planted. Besides I want to direct this one myself."

"That sounds ambitious," she said.

"Oh it is." He smiled at her. "But I've been aiming for it for a long time. Usually, I just hand it all over and let others have a heyday destroying it."

"Do they really destroy it?" she asked.

"They do have a tendency to change things to meet their own ends," he admitted.

He brought the car to a halt in front of Marisa's apartment.

"This is home," she said turning toward him.

"Is it really?" he asked, his eyes taking in the white Spanish style building.

"Is it really what?" she said.

"Home?"

She shook her head. "Just temporarily. The girl who owns it is an actress. She's making a film in Spain at the moment."

"Sounds good." His lips smiled, but not his eyes.

"It's convenient," Marisa told him, "and cheap."

"Not much money?"

"Oh a bit," she said, and turned to get out of the car. He reached across her and opened the door for her. They both got out of the car. He walked with her to the door of her apartment.

"Well," he said, "it's been a pleasure. Thank you for the work."

"That's all?" she said.

He nodded. "All for now."

She felt acute disappointment. She had looked forward to her hours working with Lew. Now it would be back to the dull routine of the library and the faint hope she always held of being discovered and becoming a star.

As if sensing her disappointment Lew moved closer and put his arm around her. "I'll see you again," he reassured her, and before she could object, he kissed her firmly on the lips. Then he got back into his car and drove off down the darkened street.

Two months later Marisa was offered a part in a film called "Jeanie." It was a small budget, clichéd production about a young country girl who went to New York in search of success and fame and went home much the wiser. Because it was a well-made film, it rocketed Marisa to stardom. The offer had come out of the blue. Although Marisa hadn't seen Lew Stone again since the night he'd driven her home from the library, she knew that he must have had something to do with the offer. She wished she could thank him personally, but she had no idea where he lived.

After "Jeanie," she had been in demand by other film companies and she soon had found herself with a contract and was hard at work on another film. But when that film was completed, she began to find success a strain and, as she had a month before her next venture, she decided to take a much-needed holiday. The same girl, Lisa, whose apartment she was renting, had offered her the use of a beach house for a month.

I haven't even got a boy friend, Marisa thought ruefully as she packed for her vacation at the beach. All the men in her life had been just friends or brief acquaintances. So much for the glamorous life of a movie star! She was always working so hard that close associations were avoided and she'd never been the type for the brief affairs that most of her colleagues indulged in. There had been numerous dates, mostly arranged for publicity, all rock stars and actors at the pinnacle of their own careers, but not one man, however handsome, had managed to capture her heart. But one could, her subconscious always argued, and she had been forced to remember clear gray eyes, a startling white smile, and the pressure of firm lips against hers and a promise to see her again. A promise Lew Stone had never fulfilled.

It had been late afternoon by the time she arrived at Lisa's beach house. She'd been to the house once before for a party and knew her way around. It didn't take her long to get unpacked, check the refrigerator, and make a list of groceries she needed.

She drove to the nearest store and purchased the items on her list. As she approached the beach house again, she noticed a gray Jaguar parked outside. Maybe a friend of Lisa's, she thought.

Carrying the bags of food up the wooden steps, she stopped in surprise. Llewellyn Stone was leaning casually against the doorway.

"Hi," he said, his teeth white against his dark tan.

"How did you know?" she asked, her heart thumping erratically. For this man, she'd had more than a dozen restless nights.

"Word gets around in this town," he told her, and made a movement toward her. "Here, let me." He swung the bags of food out of her arms leaving her to dig in her purse for the front door key.

He followed her into the house.

"Lisa's husband is a friend of mine," he explained. "He mentioned you were here. I hope I'm not intruding?"

"No, of course not," she shrugged as he put the groceries on the kitchen counter.

He was wearing a pair of faded denim jeans that fit snugly against his muscular body. His well-washed denim shirt was rolled up at the sleeves showing off tanned forearms. A silver chain, with a medallion attached, hung from his neck. She couldn't read the inscription.

"I know you've come here for a rest," he said, as Marisa began to unpack the groceries. "But I had to see you again." His eyes smouldered. "Did you want to see me again?" he asked huskily.

She nodded, not trusting herself to speak, or to hold the carton of eggs. She put them down on the counter, hoping he had not noticed her shaking hands.

"You took your time," she said at last.

"I told you I was in New York."

"All that time?"

"No I'll admit that, but I knew you were busy. I should say congratulations. It looks like you've made it."

She smiled slightly. "Thanks to you I presume?"

"I put in a word, honey," he said.

"Then I'll thank you profusely," she told him, "it's made my dream."

"Good." He smiled at her. She noticed that the kitchen was almost dark now because the sun had gone down. Lew was standing on the other side of the room. She could feel the strong magnetic force of his body as though he were beside her and touching her. The feeling terrified Marisa. Only when she was acting had she felt emotion as powerful as this.

"Would you like to stay for a meal?" she asked.

"I'd like that," he said, moving to flick on the light and breaking the spell between them.

He helped her prepare steaks and a salad and they ate sitting in comfortable armchairs in front of a log fire.

The coffee was being kept warm by the side of the fire. Marisa took up the pot and poured it into their two mugs. Lew picked up his coffee, smiling at her through the firelight. She felt a glow of happiness and contentment such as she'd never felt before except when working. Only then did she feel truly alive. But that night—that night she felt warm and alive.

"Did I read in your biography somewhere that you were from Canada?" Lew asked as he sipped his coffee.

She nodded. "I haven't been home for a few years though," she said. "How about you? Are you from California?"

"No. I'm also Canadian. I've been here a few years though," he told her.

"I suppose you've made your fortune here?" She smiled, the flickering logs picking out the highlights in her blond hair and emphasizing the golden tint of her skin. She was wearing a white silk shirt with her blue jeans and the pearly material shimmered in the firelight.

"Almost," he sighed slightly. "It wasn't easy though. A lot of hard work and long nights."

"As I've found out," Marisa told him ruefully. "Fame and fortune don't come easily."

"No they don't," he said, and put down his mug to tend to the fire, so that it blazed with sparks.

"The fire's beautiful," Marisa whispered, watching his powerful body outlined by the blaze of light. She wished that he would touch her and let her feel his lips against hers as he'd done so briefly that night outside her apartment.

The emotion she felt at this thought was so heady that she stood up to get hold of herself and walked away from the heat of the fire. But Lew was behind her, lifting the hair from the side of her neck, moving his mouth against her skin. She stirred in his arms so that she was facing him, to give him her willing mouth, her fingers moving convulsively against the rough denim material of his shirt.

His hands sought the smoothness of her skin beneath her silk blouse, moving upward to cup her breasts. Then he lowered his lips to their silky softness. She could feel him trembling while her own body felt like a quivering uncontrollable mass as her fingers clutched the taut skin of his waist.

Then he lowered her to the fluffy sheepskin rug by the roaring fire. His body was heavy and demanding, responding in passionate ardor as she arched herself against him, only knowing that she needed a physical satisfaction from this man that she'd needed from no other.

And then as he moved from her for a moment, she wondered what she was doing. Wantonly giving herself to a man who was at least ten years her senior, experienced, worldly. A man she really knew nothing about. Only that his name had appeared on the credits of many powerful, disturbing films. A man who might be married, might have children. A man who was lowering his hard muscular frame against her once more to claim only one thing.

"No!" She heard herself scream the word. She was

released abruptly from a warm passionate embrace. Feeling cold and numb, she rolled over toward the dying embers of the fire.

There was a long silence before Lew spoke softly, almost menacingly, "We had names for girls like you when I was a teen-ager."

Marisa moved on the sheepskin rug to face him. He was standing in the shadows, his shirt discarded in a heap beside her. Perspiration made his tanned skin glisten.

"Next, you'll tell me you're a virgin," he said caustically, bending over to pick up his shirt.

"I haven't—" she began to say.

"Oh come on." He slipped into the shirt and began to button it. "That's how you get on in this business."

Marisa felt some life return to her body.

"Well I happen to have gotten this far on my own," she told him angrily, standing up.

"You think so?" He tucked the shirt into the waistband of his jeans. "You'd still be slinging books in that library if I hadn't put in a word for you."

"And you want your payment, is that it?" she snapped. All the emotion she'd expended had boiled into frustrated anger. "I don't go in for one-night stands and brief affairs. I'm sorry."

"So am I," Lew told her coolly. "It wouldn't have been that brief actually. I've had some sleepless nights over you. Tonight I probably won't be able to sleep either."

Neither would she, she thought, and nearly discarded all her morals, by flinging herself in his arms, but instead, she drew the edges of her blouse tighter together to hide her nakedness.

"I would have thought waking up in each other's arms with the surf pounding against the shore would have appealed to your sense of the dramatic," Lew told her.

"Don't!" She let out a strangled sob.

He laughed grimly, "So you have been thinking the same way I have."

"I think you should leave," Marisa told him.

He plunged his hands into the back pockets of his faded jeans. "I guess I should. I had intended to stay a week, but I don't fancy the rug in front of a burnt out fire."

"Where will you go?" she asked.

"Home," he said. "I've got a perfectly good house in Beverly Hills."

"What about your wife?" she asked. One way to get some information out of him, she thought, just come right out and ask.

"Wife?" He looked genuinely startled. "I haven't got a wife. You don't mean you didn't come across because you thought I had a wife?"

"No." She shook her head in case he tried to make love to her again and this time she knew she wouldn't have the strength to push him away. "I just wondered."

"Well I haven't got a wife. I've come close a few times I'll admit, but so far I've managed to stay free."

"Then you'd better leave," Marisa told him. "That way you'll be free again."

"Sure." He looked at her for a long moment. "Thanks for the hospitality." The door slammed and she heard the Jaguar start up and crunch up the driveway and then move quietly away on the smoothness of the main road.

It had been a long month for Marisa. She supposed it was a rest, but her mental state ran in discord against her physical state and the well-being she felt in her limbs from swimming and walking along the beach was belied by sleepless nights and lack of appetite.

She found herself actually glad to get back to the apartment and begin work on her next film. She immersed herself completely in the dramatic part she had to play, so that when she arrived home late each evening, she was exhausted and would just throw herself into bed to sleep. It wasn't that she thought of Lew continuously with pain, but there had been something strong and magnetic about the man that seemed to fill a void in her life, a void she'd never noticed until she'd met him. Maybe she should have given him a chance and endured a love affair with him. But *endured* was the wrong word. To have a love affair with Lew Stone would raise her life to its highest plateau.

She had been thinking along those lines when she came home one evening and found Lew outside her apartment.

"What are you doing here?" she asked after she'd produced her key and opened the door. He seemed to make a habit out of turning up at her door.

"What a greeting," he said, following her in and closing the door behind him. He unbuttoned his leather jacket and looked around.

"What do you want?" she asked, enjoying the luxury of seeing his broad frame again.

"What do you think I want?" he said, his eyes cool and questioning.

"I wouldn't know," she told him. "I mean I've not

seen hide nor hair of you for months and now you turn up like—"

"Like what?" His lips curved into a grin. "Methinks the lady doth protest too much."

Marisa's heart pounded erratically and she dropped her eyes from his gaze.

"Did you enjoy your lonely vacation Marisa?"

"I had a wonderful time," she told him. "I had a good rest. I swam, I walked—"

"Alone?"

"I'm quite content with my own company," she said. "Not every woman must be mauled by a man to be happy."

"Mauled?" He sighed and glanced around her apartment. "I thought you had moved. I was surprised."

"Why should I move?"

"Because you're a star, Marisa. You don't have to live in junk like this."

"It isn't junk," she said, but she knew he was right. She should be right up there, living up to her image.

"Besides," he went on, "it isn't safe; anyone can get to your door."

She had had a few problems with rambunctious fans. A couple of nights she'd stayed with a friend, unable to get to her front door without being molested.

"Well, am I right?" he said, walking toward the window with its peeling, wood trim. He looked out. Tall and imposing in denim jeans and a navy shirt under the leather jacket. "It's a lousy area too," he muttered.

"Have you quite finished?" she asked.

He shook his head. "Not really," he said smiling. "But it'll do for the moment. How about a drink?"

"I only have wine."

"Then coffee'll do," he told her.

Glad to escape him if only for a brief moment, she went into the kitchen and prepared the coffee, but he joined her, leaning against the door frame. He'd taken off his leather jacket and swung it from his fingers.

"You're certainly not living like a star. What happens to all the money?"

"I'm saving it."

"What for?"

"I have nothing to spend it on."

He glanced around. "I think maybe a new apartment might be in order."

"You've already made your point," she told him acidly. What right had he to come into her life and act as though he had some authority over her!

The coffee was ready. He took the tray from her and carried it through to the living room and put it on the table. Then he flung his jacket on the back of a chair and made himself comfortable on her sofa. He patted the space beside him.

"Come and tell me what you've been doing."

"Why should I?" She stood firm, still annoyed at his proprietorial air. Then she realized that if she wanted a cup of coffee, she would have to do as he said. She went and perched beside him.

"That's better," he told her, smiling.

She sipped her coffee. "Well what have you been doing?" she asked, wishing that his thigh wouldn't brush hers as he leaned forward to stir sugar and cream into his coffee.

"Writing," he said, "as usual. What about you?"

"Another film," she told him.

"Good," he nodded. "I suppose it helps to block out reality."

"Acting is my life," she told him. "Now will you stop insulting me."

His gray eyes roamed over her slim figure in blue jeans and cream silk smock. "Not until you tell me why you look all washed out?"

"I've been working hard," she said. "Very hard, as a matter of fact." He was disconcerting her, sitting here beside her emanating virility. It made her dreams of the last weeks seem puny in comparison. And she had dreamed of him . . .

The back of his hand touched her cheek and trailed to caress her neck and her throat. "Like that?" he asked huskily.

She nodded unable to stop herself. Her eyes focused on his knee.

"I was in London recently," he said, "and you know what I did. I went and saw a couple of your movies. They were playing as a double matinee. Stupid, eh?"

"Stupid," she echoed. His hand plunged lower, caressing the mound of her breast.

"I didn't like the scene at the beach," he said. "Afterward I realized that what we had was more than just material for an affair. Marry me, Marisa?"

"What?" she asked, still not looking at him.

"Marry me?"

She glanced up at him, and his eyes were full of warmth.

"Well?" he urged.

"You want to marry me?"

"I've said it twice," he told her, sounding amused. "I'm not saying it again. What do you think?"

"I—" She shook her head, confused. She loved him. She'd discovered that in the month she'd had alone at the beach.

Then his lips moved toward hers. As their kiss deepened, Marisa found that she had no defense against him. He had aroused the passion that she had tried so desperately to suppress.

He had asked her to marry him. She would do so. She knew for her there was no other choice . . .

Chapter Three

The ringing of the telephone woke Marisa. Sleepily, she edged herself across the bed and picked up the receiver from the phone on the bedside table.

"Marisa, it's John."

"You woke me up," she told him, yawning. "Is it late?"

"Almost ten. You should be working, sweetheart. You're getting lazy."

She smiled to herself. "What do you want?"

"I want you to come up to my office so that I can persuade you to do 'The Rain Lady.'"

"John, you said you'd give me more time to think."

"You asked for another night and you've had it," John told her. "You promised," he added.

She sighed. "Oh, okay, but only because I want to cadge another lunch out of you."

"You'll get lunch when you've signed the contract."

"I'm not promising John. John!" she called into the receiver, but he had hung up. Sleeping until all hours was lazy, she knew that, but what could she do? She'd tried for a regular job, but acting experience wasn't typing and filing and that's where most opportunity lay.

She took a shower and dressed in a cotton skirt and blouse both in a musty shade of pink. Then, adding a pair of wedge sandals in the same color, she examined her reflection in the full-length mirror in her bedroom. She felt reasonably pleased with her appearance, except for a slight heaviness around her eyes caused by a restless, dream-filled night. She picked up her purse and went down in the elevator to the parking garage to get her car.

If only John had some work for her that didn't involve Lew Stone, she thought, as she drove to the main road. She wasn't afraid of acting again. But then what was she afraid of? Surely not Lew! She must be immune by now. Maybe she should do the job, just to prove it to herself.

The streets of the city were crowded with traffic, shoppers, and office workers out on coffee breaks, but Marisa managed to find a parking spot in a side street lot before making her way up to John's office.

John's secretary, Lucille, was sipping on a cup of coffee. She asked Marisa if she wanted one. Marisa declined and went straight through to John's office.

She recognized the broad shoulders outlined against John's beige drapes even before she had a chance to register who it was. And when the man turned around, she saw Llewellyn Stone.

Three years hadn't altered him much. His hair was still crisp and curly, slightly shorter than before, with a smattering of gray. His lean face was tanned, the addition of lines around his mouth and eyes giving him a distinguished maturity. His body was obviously still in peak condition, the muscles of his stomach hard and flat beneath the slim fitting clothes he wore.

"Hi," he said softly, raising an eyebrow, a hint of irony in his tone.

"Where's John?" she mouthed, her voice barely a whisper.

"He stepped out for a while." Lew Stone moved forward toward John's desk. His suit was of the finest gray corduroy and he wore a maroon shirt unbuttoned at the neck. His medallion glittered at his throat. When their intimacy had allowed her to get close and touch the medallion, he had told her it was an emblem crafted for him by a native of some country on his travels. It meant love.

Marisa breathed deeply, trying to maintain her sanity.

"He can't do this to me," she said.

"Can't do what?" Lew asked.

"Leave me with you."

"What do you think I'm going to do to you? Rape you?"

"No." She lowered her eyes so as not to meet his enigmatic, gray stare.

"John told me that you'd refused the part of Marion. I want to know why."

"You know why," she told him.

"Then I must be obtuse because, knowing your financial situation, as Benton describes it, I can't see why you would refuse."

"My financial situation has nothing to do with you."

"You think not?" He took two long strides toward her. "Even though you walked out on me, you're still my wife. You're still my responsibility."

"Then I'm surprised you haven't found me before," she told him.

"Not for lack of looking, sweetheart," he said nastily. "You hid yourself cleverly and Benton took a lot of beating down."

"Your price probably got so high he couldn't resist," she taunted. "Isn't that the way you play your game?"

Lew turned away, thrusting his hands in the pockets of his pants. "I didn't come up here to have a domestic argument," he said, "I came to offer you the part of Marion in 'The Rain Lady.'"

"And I'm declining that offer," she said to his broad back.

He turned abruptly. "Could John have persuaded you?"

"Maybe." She lowered her eyelashes so that her eyes were just a mere flash of blue.

"I see," he said. 'Then I suppose I have to bare my soul. John doesn't know it, but I've been supplying the cash to pay for your apartment, your car," his hand swung toward her, "your clothes, the lot."

Marisa's breath caught in her throat. Then Lew must have known her whereabouts for quite a while.

"I don't understand," she said.

"I don't expect you to. I approached John with 'The Rain Lady' script some time ago. I wanted you for Marion. He said you were out of commission, I think those were his words. I did some scouting around and found that Benton was heavily in debt mostly on account of you, my love, so I started a monthly check for royalties for some fictitious film you were supposed to have done. Benton bought it."

"That's not fair."

Of course it's fair." Lew flicked the drapes with his fingers, "You're putting the poor man out of business. As most of his financial problems stem from you, and as you are my wife, I'm paying up like a good husband."

"He doesn't know," she whispered, "I never told him."

"Neither did I, so that makes us even. I'm not particularly keen on getting too close to my wife's lovers."

Marisa hadn't the strength to argue with him, so she let the comment lie. At that moment Lucille popped her head around the office door.

"Are you sure you wouldn't want some coffee, Miss Marshall, Mr. Stone?"

"That would be nice, thanks, Lucille," Lew said.

"Lucille?" Marisa stopped John's secretary from leaving. "When will John be back?"

"He's out all day," Lucille told her, and left to get the coffee.

"So you're stuck with me," Lew said. "Now let's talk business."

He walked over to John's desk where the contract in the brown envelope had been placed yesterday. Lucille brought in two cups of coffee and left them on the desk.

"Thanks," Lew said, smiling at Lucille so that she smiled back coyly at him as she left the room.

So he hadn't lost his charm, Marisa thought as she went over to the desk for her coffee. She didn't really want any, but it was something to do if she had to spend time with Lew. She felt as though she'd been led into a very well laid trap and by the look of things, especially her financial situation, she had no choice but to accept the part of Marion.

Lew sat down at John's desk and stirred some sugar into his cup of coffee.

"Why don't you join me?" he said, indicating that she take the chair opposite.

With a sigh, she sat down and carried the cup and saucer to her lap, not surprised to find that she was shaking.

"We're going to have to be civilized about this, you know," Lew told her. His eyes narrowed slightly. She couldn't read their expression.

"I don't intend to be any other way," Marisa said.

"Good." He flipped open the brown envelope and took out the contract. "Have you read this?"

She shook her head.

"Damn," he said under his breath.

"Well why should I have? I don't want the part." Marisa slammed her cup of coffee on the desk so hard that some spilled over the rim.

Lew glared at her, his eyes icy. "I said *civilized.*"

"I said no."

"I hold the purse strings," he said.

"You won't let me forget that, will you?"

He shook his head, "No. Now, let's get down to business."

Marisa sat and listened. Lew's long, tanned finger pointed out the items in the contract that might need clarification, talking with the slow precision she remembered.

"It will be location work here in Canada," he told her, slipping the contract back into the envelope. "I have a house up north that I want to use. Trailers will be provided as living accommodation."

"When do you want to start?" Marisa asked.

"As soon as I have the okay from you. Paul Dexter will play the part of Roland."

"And what if I say no?" She challenged his gray glance with more bravery than she actually felt.

"You can't, Marisa. John's business depends on this." He drummed his fingers against the contract.

"Okay." She slumped back into her chair running a weary hand through her golden curls. "I'll do it. But not for you. For John."

He glanced down so that she couldn't see his eyes. "That's fine," he told her coolly, and got up from the desk holding out his hand. "Let's shake on that then."

She placed her hand into his and it reminded her of their wedding day when she'd given him her hand with such trust.

His fingers caressed hers lightly. "Shall we go for lunch?" he asked, before he released her hand.

"Lunch isn't necessary," she told him, the pressure of his grip still tingling her fingers. "I'll do it without any further persuasion."

"I wasn't considering any more persuasion. I was thinking more in the vein of a reunion," he said, watching her closely.

"Reunion?" she repeated dumbly.

"Yes." His smile was thin. "So that we can now discuss our divorce."

Chapter Four

Divorce. The word seemed to spin around inside her head as she smiled woodenly at Lucille and followed Lew to the elevator. As they stood waiting for it to arrive, she watched her husband. She looked at the expensive black leather boots, the long muscled legs in the close fitting corduroy pants, held in place by a low slung leather belt, the maroon shirt that tugged across his chest muscles, the medallion resting against his dark chest hair. Finally, she met his eyes.

"Have I got a hair out of place?" he asked, it was the closest she'd been to him since they'd met again. She noticed lines of fatigue around his eyes and mouth.

She shook her head. "No."

The elevator arrived and he ushered her on with an impersonal hand placed at her waist. Through the thin cotton of her blouse it felt like a hot iron. She was glad when they were out in the brilliant sunshine of the summer day, away from the stifling intimacy of the elevator.

He took her to a small Italian restaurant. They sat in a booth near the back of the room. When the waiter came, Marisa ordered spaghetti. Lew ordered lasagna and a bottle of wine.

"Well, how have you been?" Lew asked, when the waiter had left them.

"Not bad," she lied. "How about you?"

"Fine," he said politely. Then, "What's Benton to you?"

"I thought you'd guessed that," Marisa told him recklessly.

He gave her a narrowed look. "Lover?" he questioned.

"Friend," she said.

"And lover?" he persisted.

"If you want," she shrugged. Let him think what he wanted of her, she didn't care.

"He kept you out in the cold for a while," Lew said.

"With my permission," she snapped, before she could stop herself.

"Why?"

"Because I needed a break. Acting isn't the easiest career in the world. It's emotionally exhausting."

"Was that all?"

"Of course."

He examined the red checkered tablecloth. "Three years is a long break."

She didn't have to answer that because the waiter arrived with the wine and a basket of hot rolls.

"Well?" Lew said, when the waiter left them.

"Well, what?"

"Why three years?"

"You're persistent, I'll say that for you." She took a roll and broke it in half more for something to do than from a feeling of hunger. "Maybe I had more interesting things to do than work."

"Maybe you did." His eyes moved over her, cool and calculating. "Maybe Benton makes an interesting distraction, although I can't see why."

"No you couldn't see that any other man would prove attractive," she said in low, angry tones. "John is kind, considerate and *trustworthy*."

"Until today, when he coerced you into coming to his office."

"Maneuvered by you, no doubt," she said, wanting to wipe away his mirthless smile.

"Oh, I admit to having some bearing on it," he told her. Then his expression softened slightly. "I wanted to see you again, Marisa. It's been a long time."

Surprised by the sincerity of his tone, she found herself floundering. "I can't think why."

"No maybe not," he sighed. "I don't think you've ever understood my motives."

She laughed harshly, "You have the most basic motive—lust," she said.

"Whatever." He shrugged, his eyes growing cool again.

Marisa was glad that the waiter chose that time to arrive with their meal, but all she could do was move the spaghetti around and around on her plate.

Lew didn't seem hungry either. He only ate a roll

and part of the lasagna. He drank half the bottle of wine in silence. It was a relief when he suggested that they should leave the restaurant.

"I'll drive you home," he told her when they were once more out in the heat of the day.

"I've got my own car."

"Are you sure?" He looked down at her, his fingers linked in the leather belt at his hips.

"Don't worry I'm not going to escape," she said.

"I hope not. John'll have all the information ready for you tomorrow. Just give him a call."

"I will." She licked her dry lips, wishing she'd had more of the wine at lunch.

Lew produced a business card. "I'm staying at this hotel if you need me. The number's there."

"Why should I need you?" She stared at the card.

"To discuss our divorce," he told her. "We do have to talk about it, you know."

"But what's there to talk about?"

"Some kind of settlement," he said softly.

She still stared at the black embossed card, "But there were no kids, no home, no—"

"No," he sighed and looked away. People had to walk around them where they stood on the sidewalk.

"Then what's there to settle?" Marisa asked.

"Something for you," he said.

"I don't really want anything, Lew," she told him honestly, because she wasn't that kind of woman. She wouldn't want to bleed him dry.

"This isn't the place," he chided.

"Okay." She tried to smile. "Thanks for everything anyway . . ."

He smiled too, but it was more like a grimace.

"Why don't you come and see me tomorrow morning before you go to see Benton?" he suggested.

She agreed. She might as well get this over with now. She didn't want any emotional turbulence to distract her from her work.

"Room six hundred," he said, and turned abruptly. She was left watching his tall figure move away through the crowd.

Chapter Five

Marisa slept that night. Not through peace of mind, but from the sheer physical exhaustion of pacing the floor throughout the afternoon and most of the evening. The meeting with Lew after three years separation had shaken her up more than she cared to admit. The thought of divorce had often flitted through her mind. She knew that, at one point or other in her life, she would have had to contact Lew to sever their relationship. He might want to get married again. That was probably the reason he'd come to her now. And as for herself? Maybe one day she would also want to remarry, but the thought of sharing the intimacies she'd shared with Lew with anyone else, seemed almost ludicrous . . .

They had gotten married just three days after he proposed; a secret wedding ceremony in San Francisco, with only Mark Lawson, Lew's best friend and business partner, and Mark's wife, Barbara, as witnesses.

"I don't want the media getting hold of this," Lew had said. "I want to keep you to myself."

It had all seemed rushed and almost irrational. After dinner with Barbara and Mark, Marisa and Lew had gone to Lew's Beverly Hills home. As Lew had to be in New York in a few days, and Marisa was in a film, they had scant time for a honeymoon.

Lew had shown her the master bedroom and put her luggage down beside the bed. Then muttering something about locking up and getting a drink, he had disappeared leaving her alone.

Marisa hadn't been quite sure what was going to happen next. The ease they'd felt with each other at the library seemed lost now. It was as though their first throes of passion had never been. Since the time she'd agreed to marry him, he had been exceptionally cool. Even the kiss he had given her in the little church had been tight-lipped and unemotional. And although he had watched her carefully throughout the remainder of the day, his conversation had always included Barbara and Mark. The faint, gnawing suspicion she had, that he didn't return the deep feelings she felt for him, had already begun to haunt her. But then, she told herself sternly, would a man get himself entangled with a woman for any other reason than love? Not a man as successful and powerful as Llewellyn Stone! If it was just sex he wanted, there must be hundreds of willing women out there. He only had to smile at them persuasively.

With a shrug, Marisa went to her suitcase and took

out the sexy blue nightgown that she'd purchased. Would Lew like it? She stood with it in front of the mirror and smiled to herself a little mistily. Should she have waited for someone younger like herself, inexperienced and full of the wonder of first love, not jaded as her husband seemed to be? She sighed heavily, and then jumped as she saw Lew's reflection in the mirror.

"Sorry," he said, "I didn't mean to scare you." He'd discarded the black jacket that matched his suit trousers and hung it from his fingers over his shoulder. His tie was unknotted and his white shirt unbuttoned.

She held up the flimsy nightgown. "I was just admiring my trousseau," she told him nervously.

His eyes glinted, "Are you going to put it on so that I can admire it also?" he asked.

"Of course." she said, but she didn't feel so secure inside.

He stretched luxuriously, casting the suit jacket across the back of a chair. "Well it's been a long hard day." He eyed her with a smile. "You seem to have come off okay."

"Not bad," she murmured.

"How does it feel being Mrs. Stone?"

"Overwhelming," she told him breathlessly, and then watched with eyes wide as he proceeded to take off his tie and shirt and throw them to join the jacket.

He unbuckled the belt of his pants and stepped out of them, almost naked now, except for a brief pair of underpants that looked like swimwear. He hung his suit in the closet.

"I've cleared a side here for you," he said. "There's

more space in the dressing room." He pointed to a door, "Maybe you'd like to change there?"

She was winding her nightgown around her fingers. He'd obviously seen her distress. She almost ran into the other room.

She undressed in a shaking hurry. He was so cool, absolutely unabashed about her seeing him half naked. Probably there had been so many women in his life that it was normal for him. But not for her. She'd never even been in a bedroom with a man before.

Finally, dressed in the sheer negligee, her stomach wound into tight knots, she wandered timidly into the bedroom. But Lew wasn't there. It was almost with relief that she began to brush her hair in long, soothing strokes. The nightgown didn't cover much, she thought wryly. All the soft curves of her body were outlined through the transparent material.

"You have beautiful hair." Lew's voice floated to her softly. She turned around to look at her husband. He was leaning casually against the door frame, a white towel around his waist contrasting with the darkness of his skin. He'd obviously just taken a shower. Probably to give her time.

The eyes observing her were dark and unfathomable.

"You're jumpy, Marisa," he said.

"A little." She put the brush on the dresser and picked it up again.

"I wish I could say it was my first time also, although it is my first attempt at marriage. Maybe that counts for something."

"Maybe," she murmured, her lips dry and her breath coming in small gulps.

He came into the room, and moved toward her.

With his fingers he traced the smooth skin of her face and neck beneath her hair, rubbing his thumb against her neck.

"Don't be afraid," he said.

"I'm not—" she started to say, but his lips were upon hers, moving with an expert skill that aroused the desire kindling inside her. His mouth moved down her neck, trailing to the edge of her nightgown. He pulled down the straps exposing her breasts and his lips and hands began to play havoc with her senses. She pushed herself against his hard muscular thighs feeling his arousal, knowing that she loved him more than life itself.

He lifted her and took her to the bed. He stood before her and she felt cold, needing his powerful body to be pressed against her again. Then he removed the towel from around his waist and she gave way to the full turbulence of his lovemaking . . .

Chapter Six

The elevator whisked Marisa to the sixth floor of one of the most expensive hotels in Toronto and deposited her on thick piled carpet in the corridor. She walked to number Six Hundred and knocked on the door. There was no answer. She rapped again, louder, and Lew put his head around the corner.

"Sorry," he said, opening the door, his gray eyes sleepy and his hair ruffled, "I was still sleeping."

She noticed that he was wearing a short navy terry cloth robe tied loosely at the waist, displaying a good portion of tanned chest. His legs were also tanned, lean and muscular. Marisa felt her throat constrict. Whatever there was between them now, it didn't blot out the memories. She could remember the feel of that lean hard body against her own.

"Maybe I should come back later," she said huskily.

"No don't. This is a suite; you can wait in the living room."

She shrugged and followed him in. He gestured toward a comfortable sofa.

"Take a seat," he said. "I won't be long."

Too nervous to sit down, Marisa went to the window and looked out. Through the hazy sunshine, she could see sailing boats bobbing on Lake Ontario.

Before leaving home that morning, she had called John to tell him of her decision and had made an appointment to see him for lunch. She'd made a joke out of the methods he'd employed to get her to play the part of Marion. She did not want to condemn him for his actions. He was obviously in desperate financial straits, and, as Lew had pointed out, she was mainly the cause. She could hardly blame him for his action.

"Wish you were out sailing on the lake?" Lew said behind her.

She turned in surprise because he'd been quicker than she'd expected. He was wearing beige cords and a shirt patterned in small checks of brown and beige. The medallion glinted in the sun from the window. His hair was damp and smooth from the shower. There was a fresh aroma of aftershave and soap emanating from his body. She noticed the harsh lines grooving his mouth. His eyes appeared to be bloodshot.

"Sorry to have kept you," he said. Then, as if noticing her stare, he rubbed a tired hand across his brow. "I met a friend last night and over-imbibed, I'm afraid. You'll have to excuse the frazzled appearance. Would you like some coffee?"

"Please," she nodded.

He left her to go to the telephone and order coffee. He put his hand over the receiver, "Have you had breakfast?" he asked.

She shook her head. Before hanging up, he ordered toast and jam to go along with the coffee.

Then, he moved toward her to pick up a package of small cigars from the coffee table and put one between his lips. He lit it with a gold cigarette lighter that he took from his pocket.

"You never smoked before," she said, before she could stop herself.

"There's a lot you don't know about me," he said, sighing. "Are you going to stand up all morning or do you want to sit down?" Wordlessly, Marisa sank down on the sofa.

"That's better. You were making me nervous."

Marisa raised an eyebrow. She couldn't remember a time when he'd been nervous.

Catching her skeptical look, Lew shrugged his shoulders before answering the knock on the door. It was their coffee and toast. Lew had the man put it on the coffee table. Marisa was surprised to find herself hungry in spite of the uncomfortable situation.

Lew sat down beside her. The soft couch gave way to his weight and she sank further back.

"I presume you want a divorce?" he said.

"Of course," she told him, but as she mouthed the words, she wasn't sure that she really meant them. To be divorced meant to be completely severed. Not even joined by a name and a wedding band.

"Then I'll go ahead with it," he said bleakly. "Or would you rather?"

"You can probably pull more strings than I," she told him, putting her cup and saucer on the coffee table.

"I'll make sure there's a monthly check for you in the settlement," he said. "It'll pay your rent and any extras."

"You don't have to, Lew."

He got up so abruptly that she nearly fell off the sofa. "I do, damn you," he said.

Marisa stood up too. "Money," she murmured, "it cures all ills." She turned away from him.

"I just don't want you to be left without any," he told her. "Understand?"

She turned back to look at him, but this time there were tears in her eyes. She was still vulnerable to him, even though she had thought herself cured. All the time she was still linked to him by name, she still bore hope, but the sinking feeling that was overcoming her now, was the thought of not having that link. Just a check once a month.

She noticed how tired he looked and had the urge to lift her hand and caress his face with her fingers. She resisted, however, and looked down at the toes of her tan leather sandals and the hem of her yellow cotton dress.

"Do you want more coffee?" Lew asked, finally breaking the strained silence.

She shook her head. "No," and then, impulsively, "you seem tired."

He pushed at his hair now drying and beginning to curl. "Working too hard probably," he told her.

"You always worked too hard." There was still the hint of tears in her eyes, making her voice husky.

He raised his eyebrows, "Maybe I did," he said.

"Well," she said with forced brightness. "I suppose I'd better go now. It's settled, we'll get a divorce." Her voice trembled and she swallowed hard. *Don't let me break down,* she prayed. *Let me get away from the hard probing coldness of his eyes.*

"Marisa?" He was close to her now and his fingers gripped her arm.

"What, Lew?" She looked up at him and knew it was a mistake. His eyes were no longer cold, no longer probing, but smouldering with desire.

His fingers tangled amongst her curls. "You cut your hair," he murmured almost to himself rather than to her. "You had such smooth, beautiful hair."

"Please, Lew," Marisa's breath caught in her throat.

Then she stood, as though mesmerized, while his hand moved toward her neck and her throat. When their lips met, the kiss seemed to go on forever. Memories streamed through Marisa's consciousness remembering other times in his arms. Always between them there had been this intensity, this force. Then he was covering her face with kisses, his breathing as uneven as her own. His hands moved to her hips and pulled her closer. She could feel the entire outline of his body through her thin cotton dress as he kissed her again with hardening passion.

Then through the floating sensation, the urgency, she remembered why they were together in this hotel room. They had been discussing their divorce, probably because he wanted to marry another woman.

"No!" She moved away from him so violently that she almost stumbled.

"Mari?" His voice was husky, his eyes glazed with passion.

"Don't touch me, Lew." She must escape him. She didn't want to be hurt again. But it had been heaven to be held by him again, to feel his kisses, the strength of his hard body. It would have been so easy to have gone into the next room with him, to his bed.

He seemed to have gained control again, although his hands were shaking as he lit one of his small cigars. "Thinking of Benton?" he asked.

"I have to have lunch with him," she murmured.

"His lovemaking can't be very satisfying. That was quite a response." Once more his eyes were icy gray. Had she imagined the smouldering desire and the uneven breathing?

"John satisfies me in every way," she snapped at him.

When she was sure her dress was buttoned evenly and her hair in order, she grabbed her handbag and left the room.

Marisa didn't remember much of her afternoon with John. Just the parts where he handed her a pen and said, "Sign here, and here, and here. Great!"

What would she be signing next? she wondered. Divorce papers. *Just sign here and you'll be free of Llewellyn Stone for life, Marisa. Free on paper, but not inside.* The familiar pain had only been dormant, waiting for him to arouse her again with his kisses and his body.

"Well I guess that's it," John said, looking pleased with himself.

"You both did a good job of persuasion," Marisa told him.

"I'm sorry, sweetheart," he sighed, "but I really had no choice."

She nodded, "I know."

"I mean an offer from someone like Llewellyn Stone can really upgrade business. He must think you're a great actress to hold out for you."

Then because she had to tell someone she said, "He felt it was his husbandly duty."

"His what?" John looked astounded.

"We're married, John. We have been for four years."

"And you never told me?"

"Why should I?"

John ran his hand through his hair, "But if I'd known. I mean I—"

"What difference would it have made?"

"I wouldn't have pushed so hard, I would have—"

"What, John? I had to see him again one day."

John sighed, "Then maybe this is for the best. Are you going to get a divorce?"

She nodded.

"I'm sorry."

"It had to come." She stood up and moved around in the room. She felt her control slipping.

"And I've precipitated it?" John said.

"Don't blame yourself," Marisa told him. She glanced at her watch. "Look I think I'll go home now. I've got a lot of work to do."

"You start Monday," John told her, a worried look on his handsome face. "Are you sure you're okay?"

"Fine." She smiled weakly.

"I'll pick you up on Monday morning and take you along to the studio."

"There's no need . . ."

"There's every need." He came around the desk, and put a comforting arm across her shoulder as she walked to the door. "Take care," he told her.

Chapter Seven

True to his word, John picked her up in his car on Monday morning to take her to the studio. Marisa felt that he didn't trust her getting there alone, even though he had the signed contract securely in his grasp. Perhaps he was right. Maybe she would have tried to edge out. Anything not to see Lew again.

John glanced at her briefly as he wound his way through the early morning, almost deserted city streets.

"Relax," he said. "You look tense."

"I am," she told him.

"There's no need to be you know. It'll all work out fine. I can feel it in my bones."

"Or in your bank account." She looked at him with a hint of mischievousness.

"Well that'll be healthier too, I can assure you. So will yours."

"I know. I'm doing it for that reason and maybe—"

"What?"

"Maybe for my self-esteem," she said.

John patted the back of her hand where it lay in her lap.

"I'm sure it'll do you a world of good. You need a chance like this. Lew Stone or no Lew Stone."

"Rich powerful men." Marisa laughed slightly, "As long as I never again fall in love with one of them."

"How about poor powerful men?"

"One in particular?" She glanced at him sideways. John had a habit of dropping his personal feelings into conversation when she least expected them.

"You know I'll marry you, as soon as you get yourself untangled from Stone," he said.

"And get yourself another divorce in a few years. No, John, wait until you meet someone who can be a complete wife to you."

"And you couldn't? You look pretty whole to me."

"You know what I mean. I'm fond of you, but love . . ."

"It comes, you know."

"I don't think so, John. Really."

"Okay." He shrugged and parked the car. "But if you ever feel the need—"

"I know, and thanks." She touched the back of his hand before getting out of the car.

They walked across the lot together. Marisa was dressed in yellow cotton slacks and a cream silk blouse with a matching yellow cotton waistcoat, the buttons left open, and a colorful scarf tied around her neck. She looked young and lovely.

John took her arm.

"Did Lew explain that the film will be shot up north somewhere around an old farmhouse? You'll get briefed today. I believe he's found the exact house that suits the ancestral home in his script," John told her.

"That sounds like Lew," Marisa said. How easy to say his name! To let it slip from her lips as though she'd never cared.

They went through the door and up a couple of steps. A man broke away from a group standing around drinking coffee from paper cups.

"John." He put out his hand. John let go of Marisa's arm to shake the man's proffered hand.

"Paul, how are you?"

"Fine." Paul's dark eyes found and rested on Marisa. "And this is Marisa?"

"None other," John said, bringing Marisa forward. "Marisa Marshall meet Paul Dexter. I used to be his agent until he became too hot for me to handle."

Paul laughed. He was obviously fully conscious of his broad, dark good looks. He shook Marisa's hand holding it a touch longer than necessary. "Glad to meet you."

"It's nice meeting you too," she said. "I saw you in 'The Extra Man.' You were excellent."

Nothing like a compliment to enlarge an actor's ego, she thought. She could almost see Paul's chest expand in the already skin-tight denim shirt. He adopted an air of modesty.

"I did my best," he said.

"It showed," she told him, acting for a fellow actor. She hadn't lost her touch there anyhow.

"I understand you're to play Marion?"

"I am," she told him. "You're Roland I believe?"

"Leading man, leading lady," John laughed. "I'm sure you'll work well together."

"I know we will," Paul told him. "Why don't you come and meet the others?"

Marisa shuddered. He even had a fake southern American accent and everyone knew he was born in Montreal. He was magnetically handsome though, so that even when his personality grated, her glance was held by his dark inscrutable eyes, smoothly tanned face and jet black hair. Even John, who was notably handsome and tall, was overshadowed. Only one man would hold his own against him—Lew Stone. She didn't see him though as she was taken over and introduced to the group of people drinking coffee.

Was this Lew's custom, to have his actors and film unit arrive on time, and then appear late himself?

"Lew'll be along shortly," said a plump, dark-haired girl, as if answering her unspoken thought. "His plane was delayed in L.A."

"L.A.?" Marisa said.

"He went back for the weekend," she told her.

"Then let's have another cup of coffee," Paul Dexter said, "while waiting for the great man."

A machine in the corner was plugged with quarters and coffee was served all round. Marisa stood, sipping her coffee, while John talked to a small, thin man with an English accent.

Then suddenly there was a silence over the group. Eyes turned toward the door as it opened. Footsteps sounded on the few steps, then across the floor.

"Morning," Lew's voice said, "sorry I was late." Icy gray eyes took in the group. He nodded as he recognized familiar faces, "Paul," he said, "how are you?"

"Fine Lew," Paul said.

"Jean?" He addressed the plump, dark-haired girl.

"Morning Lew."

"Marisa?"

She looked up, glad her paper coffee cup was empty, because she was crushing it between her fingers.

"Hello Lew," she said.

"Glad you made it."

Well, what did he think? That she'd back out at the last minute? Probably. She felt John beside her, his hand squeezing hers. She was freezing cold. Frozen by Lew's icy glance, despite the lightness of his words and the masklike smile.

"Everyone here?" Lew asked, moving toward a chair and placing a slim briefcase on it. He was wearing tight fitting black cords and a black shirt and jacket. He took off the jacket and rolled up the sleeves of the shirt, before coming over to where Marisa stood with John.

"Hi," he said to John, extending his hand. "How are you?"

"Fine, and you?" John sounded in awe of him as they shook hands.

He's just a man, Marisa wanted to yell, *just a man with faults like any other*.

"Travel battered," Lew said with a smile. "I want to thank you for producing Marisa."

"I just followed instructions," John told him.

"You did well." Lew looked around him, "Well I think we'd better get on. I've kept everyone waiting long enough."

John said good-bye to both of them, reminding Marisa to phone him if she needed a lift home in his car.

"He takes good care of you," Lew remarked. Then he said, "You look pale, what were you doing all weekend?"

"At home studying the script," she said. "At least I wasn't galavanting all over the universe."

"You look as though you had been."

"Well I wasn't. I don't have someone in every port whom I have to keep happy with evening visits."

He raised his eyebrow, "The irate wife?" he said softly." Isn't it rather late for that?"

"Don't needle me Lew," she said.

"Sorry baby," he drawled.

Marisa noticed that the rest of the crew were looking at them curiously. She indicated them with her head.

"Don't you think we'd better get on? You've kept us waiting long enough already."

"So I have. Was the wait tedious?"

"No, enjoyable. It's this conversation that's tedious," she said, walking away from him and joining the others. *That'll teach you Lew Stone.*

But she hadn't disturbed him in the least. He ambled over, thumbs hooked in the belt of his pants, and asked Jean to get him some strong coffee, then he proceeded to give instructions in cool, enunciated tones.

"I want to start early tomorrow," he said, after filling them in on technical details. "We'll rehearse down here and then go on location. The quicker we learn the sooner we start filming. Got that?"

Everyone nodded.

Lew looked around, "Anything else?" he asked.

A few had questions. He answered them swiftly.

Sandwiches were delivered for lunch. After they'd eaten, they were filled in on a few more pertinent details. At about three o'clock, Lew stood up, stretched, and looked at his watch.

"Let's call it quits," he said, rolling down the sleeves of his shirt and buttoning the cuffs. *He looks tired,* Marisa thought.

"I'll see you all here tomorrow at nine." He picked up the slim briefcase and his jacket and looked at Marisa. "Can I give you a lift?"

"No—I—" The question was entirely unexpected.

"I understood that you didn't have a car with you?"

"Yes but—"

"Oh come on, sweetheart. Don't beat around the bush. I'm tired. I've worked around the clock for two days straight. I'll drop you off home."

What else could she do? She smiled at everyone, said good night and left at Lew's side.

Outside it was hot and humid, the sky cloudy and gray. The asphalt melted beneath their feet as they walked over to a metallic gray Porsche.

Lew produced a key and opened the door. Inside, Marisa felt as though she were in the cockpit of a plane.

"Is this yours?" she indicated the car as they drove off with muted power, the engine rumbling.

"Who else's?" he asked.

She shrugged.

"I thought, as I'm going to be here for a while, I might as well set myself up with decent transportation."

"Of course," she agreed. Anyone else would have

settled for a cheap runabout, but not Lew. He purchased the most expensive, the most luxurious.

"Don't look at me like that," he said. "I'll keep it, wherever I go. I'm not that extravagant."

"I didn't think you were," she said.

"Oh no?" One eyebrow raised slightly. "Where do you live, by the way?" He seemed to be driving aimlessly.

"Actually we're going in the right direction," she told him. "It's some way yet, though."

Marisa sat back in the seat, and ran her hands over the material of her slacks on her thighs. Her hands were clammy and hot, despite the efficient air conditioning in the car.

"I saw my lawyer when I was in California," he said.

"Oh."

"He said we'll get an easy divorce, due to the long separation. You'll have to state reasons though."

"You want me to get the divorce?"

"Of course. Isn't that the polite way of doing it?"

"I never knew you to be polite," she murmured.

He smiled, "No, but I'd like to preserve your pride when it hits the papers."

"What about yours?"

"I'll survive," he said.

"This is where I'm living. The building with the white brick."

"Impressive," he said, driving off the road and up into the entrance driveway. "What floor are you on?"

"Tenth," she told him.

"I suppose you wouldn't want to invite me up to see what I'm paying for?"

"Not really," she said.

"Pity," he told her. "I'd like to see what my money's supporting."

"Then you're going to be disappointed aren't you?" She said turning toward the door to open it. He leaned across her to release the catch, brushing her breasts with his hand as he did so.

"I suppose I am," he said, watching her nervous breathing with amusement.

A horn honked behind them causing Lew to swear under his breath.

"Okay, go," he said. "I'll see you tomorrow at nine, and don't be late—Mrs. Stone," he added. He was just giving her time to get out of the car before starting the engine.

Chapter Eight

Marisa gratefully sank into a chair and sipped on the hot cup of coffee someone had handed to her. Rehearsals were almost over and most of the actors seemed to know their parts. Lew wasn't yelling quite as much as he had at first, if that was any indication, Marisa thought wryly. Patience, she knew from experience, wasn't one of his virtues. That was probably why he had undertaken this entire project himself. He had a personally hand-picked crew and cast. They were people whom he knew and had worked well with before. He showed no special attention to anyone who was working for him, treating everyone with a polite professionalism. There had been nothing in his manner to indicate that Marisa was his wife or that there had ever been any emotional attachment between them. In fact he had gone out of his way to avoid her, only talking to her when it was necessary for the job. Divorce seemed to have been forgotten, at least for the time being, but then Lew's lawyers in L.A. could be working on it. It was probably only a matter of signing a few papers and it would be over.

Not that the film would be over very quickly. On Monday they were to meet up north for the actual filming and live up there for the duration. If Lew kept his distance as he had these past weeks, Marisa felt she would have no trouble. When it was all over, she could go back to her life and begin again.

Monday was sunny, promising a hot day, when Marisa started off in her car. Despite having to work with Lew, she realized how lucky she was to be working again. She was over halfway there when she thought she'd stop for some breakfast. She was beginning to feel hungry and in need of a good hot cup of coffee. She'd been noticing the "breakfast is now being served" signs for some miles.

Seeing a small family restaurant that promised home-cooked food, she drove into the parking lot, parked the car, and went inside. A waitress seated her at a corner table by the window where she looked out across the green fields of a neighboring farm. Marisa ordered bacon and eggs, accepting a cup of coffee from the waitress while waiting for the rest of her breakfast.

She ate with more hunger than she would have credited herself with. Finally, she sat back in her seat to enjoy another cup of coffee, noticing that it was only nine o'clock. It would be easy to get to the set on time. She hadn't far to travel. The countryside outside the window was a pleasant change from high-rises and concrete. Then her heart seemed to leap in her chest and her stomach began to churn. Lew Stone's low slung sports car drew up alongside her car outside. He unfurled his long length. He was dressed casually in jeans and a shirt. Dark glasses shaded his eyes.

He came through the door and saw her right away. His lips twisted slightly. "Well, well, well," he said, moving into the chair opposite and taking off his sunglasses, "fancy meeting you here."

"Not so strange, since we're traveling in the same direction," she said, surprised at how light and normal she could sound.

He acknowledged her comment with a brief smile.

"All ready for hard work?" he asked.

"Of course, and you?" she said.

"Oh, I'm prepared." He leaned his elbow on the table. "I think rehearsals went quite well don't you?"

"Very well," she said.

"Do you feel the part's right for you?" he asked.

"Oh yes," she told him honestly. "I'm really into it."

"Good," he smiled again and then, as the waitress was waiting, he ordered bacon and eggs and coffee.

While he gave the woman his order, Marisa watched him, noticing once again how tired he looked. It wasn't just age showing in the gray that streaked his dark thick hair, or the extra lines around his eyes and mouth, but an ingrained fatigue. Perhaps his jet-setting lifestyle was proving too much for him.

"Tell me what you've been doing?" Marisa asked politely.

"Writing 'The Rain Lady' and directing a movie in England. I also spent some time in South America."

"Why South America?" she was interested.

"I had some business interests down there that have turned very profitable. Mark Lawson, remember him? He's handling it now."

"Yes I remember Mark," she said. "I think I saw your name on the credits of a television show too?"

He nodded, "And that. I haven't let the grass grow under my feet."

"You wouldn't," Marisa couldn't help herself saying and felt she deserved the rather wry smile he gave her.

The waitress brought his breakfast and he ate it hungrily. Marisa took the offer of more coffee. She couldn't just get up and leave him alone, not when they were both moving toward the same destination.

Lew glanced out the window at the green Ontario countryside. "It's good to be home for a while," he said.

"I thought L.A. was home now?" she questioned.

"I guess it is in a way," he told her. "But you know what L.A.'s like. I know too many people there."

Marisa smiled, remembering her own hectic life there.

"Besides," he went on, "I might make this my last film."

"You don't mean that?" She was truly surprised.

"Why not? I could stay at home and write books instead of film scripts." He looked amused at her surprise, "You don't believe me?"

"I can't see you retiring."

"When I was twenty, I said I would retire at forty. I might achieve my dream."

She looked across at him, studying his face. His eyes

weren't icy gray today, but warm and friendly, though guarded. "The great Lew Stone retired. I hope it'll be a good book, otherwise they'll forget you."

"They probably will anyway. Films are remembered for their actors not their script writers." He glanced at the gold watch on his wrist. "We should be off," he said, picking up her bill as well as his own.

"No need," she said, reaching out. She wanted to be independent.

"My treat," he murmured, standing up and pulling out her chair for her to stand up. Her bare arm brushed his. She could smell the stimulating aroma of his aftershave. "It's a husband's duty," he whispered, and was gone before she could retort.

Marisa watched his car disappear around the first corner, the power of the engine eating up the miles. Her car wasn't slow but it could never compare to his. Besides, why rush? She didn't particularly relish any more intimate time in his company even though she felt exhilarated. But Lew made everyone feel like that. She'd felt it these past weeks among the film crew. It was his charisma, or whatever the papers wanted to call it. He was the kind of person everyone wanted to talk to, or be seen with.

She needn't have worried about being alone with Lew again. By the time she arrived at the location, the crew were already set up and Jean had made coffee and was serving it from one of the trailers.

Marisa parked her car in the wide circular driveway of the large brick house. It was an imposing building with huge white pillars. There was a contractor's truck pulled up near the open front door. The smell of new paint floated her way as she peeped through the door. She could see a man working from a scaffolding. Another man with a hammer knelt on the stairs. She would love to look further inside, but most of the windows were shuttered. She supposed she'd get her chance soon enough.

The house had a good deal of land attached. The crew were out in the back on part of the acreage. A number of trailers were parked in a field a good distance from the house. Marisa saw Lew deep in conversation with Paul Dexter.

"Like some coffee?" Jean called to Marisa as she wandered, rather self-consciously, across the field.

"No thanks," Marisa told her, wondering where her own trailer was. She had packed a minimum amount of luggage and would fetch it from her car later when she knew where she was to sleep. She walked toward Jean.

"Everyone seems very industrious," she remarked to the plump, dark-haired girl who was preparing more coffee.

"Some of us came last night," Jean told her.

"It's beautiful out here." Marisa held her face to the warm wind, squinting a little in the sun.

"Very hot though," Jean said. "It's going to be hard work."

"I think I'll enjoy it," Marisa told her, realizing unexpectedly, that it was the truth. She left Jean and went over to where Paul Dexter, now separated from Lew, stood, talking to a group of people.

"Marisa, darling." Paul smiled as she walked up, "How are you today?"

"Fine, it's a beautiful day." She smiled at Paul and at the others.

"Are you all set?" one of the men asked. She recognized him as a cameraman.

"Not really." Marisa touched her stomach. "First morning jitters naturally."

"You'll be great," Paul assured her, "just great."

"You've probably never seen anything I've done," she teased.

"Of course I have, sweetheart. I'm one of your fans."

"Then I hope I won't disappoint you," she told him.

Everyone seemed as confident as she'd once been. After three years absence the feeling was more than just butterflies. She'd been good at rehearsals, but when she actually came under fire from the cameras, she wondered if she would have the stamina.

Lew was rounding up everyone. Marisa leaned against the trunk of a big tree and listened. The wind rustled through the leaves and the long grass What a lovely spot to be in summer or winter! She could imagine being tucked up warm and snug in front of a huge log fire in the house, while the snow piled high outside. It was the kind of home she'd always dreamed of living in, snug with husband and children. *Husband*, she thought and gazed at Lew.

He was wearing his sunglasses and had rolled up the sleeves of his shirt. The buttons were open almost to his waist. He was talking to Joanna Mason who was playing the part of Jacqueline in the film.

Lew didn't look much different from the first time Marisa had met him and he still affected her the same way. He was an incredibly sexy looking man. Marisa could see even the rather demure and married actress, Joanna Mason, reacting to him flirtatiously.

Disturbed by her feelings, Marisa stood up and walked to where some of the others were standing. Being alone with her thoughts was dangerous.

As the morning progressed Marisa noticed that Lew looked as though he would explode with anger. Paul and Joanna had messed up their opening scene again. Instead, he turned around, ran his hand across his chest beneath his shirt and said calmly, "Okay, lunch." Everyone breathed a sigh of relief. They filtered over toward Jean and the trailer where the smell of soup wafted toward them.

The afternoon went much the same as the morning. Lew got so mad that he had to walk away from them all to calm down. Paul Dexter looked sheepish and Joanna Mason seemed ready to cry.

"I thought it was perfect that last time," she said to Marisa sipping on a soft drink from a paper cup someone handed her. "He's a hard man to please."

"He's a perfectionist," Marisa told her, "that's all. But you'll get it. Wait till we've been here a few weeks."

"I hope we wrap it up quickly," Joanna said.

"I'm sure Lew does too," Marisa said, wondering why she was defending the man, but of course she couldn't belittle his working habits, whatever their personal relationship had been.

"Joanna," Lew called. "Can we try it just once more?"

Jo put her cup down. "Sure." She muttered under her breath.

They had not even completed the second half of the scene, when they had to wrap it up for supper. Marisa could see that Lew was agitated.

They all ate on trestle tables set up outside. Tension began to ease as the beer flowed. Everyone, including Lew, livened up slightly. Some of the men had brought their wives along, a couple had small children. They went to their trailers early.

Jean showed Marisa where she was to sleep.

"But it's huge," Marisa said when she saw her trailer. There was a stereo and television set, small refrigerator and stove.

"It's the most luxurious trailer here," Jean said. "Lew insisted."

"But—"

"What Lew says goes on his sets," Jean told her. "He said to get you the best."

Marisa shrugged slightly, not knowing what to say. She was still his wife after all, maybe this was one of the perks.

Jean went over and opened a door.

"There's a shower and everything here. I understand we can't use the big house quite yet. Lew is still having work done. He wants to get all the outside shots first and do the inside ones when some of the rooms are finished."

"I'm sure it's beautiful inside," Marisa said.

Jean wrinkled her nose, "It's musty and damp at the moment, but I guess, given time for the improvements, it could be nice."

"It's the kind of house I'd like to own," Marisa told her impulsively.

Jean smiled, "Well you're too late on that score; it belongs to Lew."

"It does?" Marisa was truly surprised, "Did he buy it for the film?"

"Oh I don't think so," Jean told her. She walked toward the door. "Well I'd better be going. Sleep well. Just yell if there's anything else you need."

"I will," Marisa said, and waved before closing the door after the girl.

Marisa walked around the trailer, checking the cupboards in the kitchen, noting that they were stocked with canned goods. She decided to run out to the car and get her belongings. Then she would make herself some coffee and go over the script.

She went down the trailer steps. The site was empty of people; lights reflected from inside the trailers. She noticed a light on inside the house in one of the back rooms. Was Lew living there? If he owned the house, he probably was. She wondered how long he'd owned it and decided she would ask him, then thought better of it. The less they said of a personal nature, the better. She'd keep away from him as much as possible. Who cared if he owned a nice old house like this?

It was a warm evening with a streaked red sky. She could hear the crickets singing as she walked across the grass. In spite of everything, Marisa was happy at the prospect of spending a few weeks in these quiet, peaceful surroundings.

The graveled driveway crunched beneath her feet as

she went over to her car and unlocked the door. She took out her small suitcase and another bag containing makeup and toiletry items.

"Need any help?" Marisa looked up to see Lew coming out of the front door of the house and across the driveway.

"Not really," she told him. He came closer.

"Everything okay?" he asked. "Accommodations to your liking?"

"Did you expect it not to be?" she asked him. "You've obviously laid on all the extras."

"I wouldn't want you to be dissatisfied."

"Money doesn't always buy satisfaction," she told him, locking the car door, and moving to pick up her luggage.

"It helps though." He moved in front of her, and picked up her cases. "I'll take these over."

"There's no need."

He began to walk across the pathway to the side of the house. She had to run to catch up.

"Really, Lew, you don't have to do this! I'm quite capable."

"You probably are," he said, looking down at her, "but you've got lots of hard work ahead of you, I want you in good shape. You look tired. I don't want that."

"What am I supposed to look like?" she demanded. "After all, you have suddenly come back and disrupted my nice, peaceful existence."

"How peaceful do you think it would be to have your creditors knocking at your door forcing you to find cheaper accommodations?"

"That would never happen."

"Don't be so sure," he snapped, still walking so fast

that she found herself a few paces behind his broad back and long lean legs, clad in faded denims.

"Do you have to walk so fast?"

He slowed down. "Sorry," he said.

"You think you've just come along in the nick of time don't you? Saved me from a fate worse than death?"

He gave her an exasperated look, "I don't think anything of the kind. I'm just not sure that you could handle living on the edge of poverty."

"I've lived on the edge of poverty before. I'm quite used to saving and stinting."

"That's why you're living in that fancy apartment and cruising around in that expensive car?"

"What about you? You don't stint and save either."

"No, but I can afford to pay my bills." He dumped her luggage down beside the trailer steps, and regarded her coolly, the planes of his face harsh beneath the electric light shining outside the trailer door.

"Maybe John didn't handle my money correctly," she said.

He sighed, "Yes he did. He's quite honorable you know. He showed me the books. Everything was in order."

"Then I suppose I have to thank you for what you've done for me," she said.

"I'd do it for anybody," he told her off-handedly. "Why don't you get to bed? You look awful. I don't want any more days like today."

Marisa's lips trembled. How could he stand there and insult her with one remark after another? Today's fiasco on the set hadn't involved her. If he was angry, why didn't he go and insult those who had caused his anger? She went up the steps to the trailer door, opened it, and bundled her luggage through.

Lew stood and watched until she was finished. "Good night," he said. "Try to be in shape for tomorrow."

She slammed the door in his face.

Marisa stood on the other side of the door, her breath coming heavily. Why didn't he stop irritating her and leave her alone? After all, she'd agreed to the divorce and the film. She unpacked, undressed, then took a shower in the neatly appointed bathroom, glad of the preferential treatment that gave her the modern devices. Maybe she was spoiled. Perhaps Lew was right.

Slipping on a blue silk robe, she filled the kettle, setting it on the little gas stove. She sat down at the table with the script in front of her. Despite all the agitation she felt, she had to get down to work. After a while, a hot cup of coffee in front of her, and part way through the first scene, she calmed down sufficiently to begin to go through her lines.

Chapter Nine

"Okay cut," Lew yelled. "We've got most of it. Let's have something to eat. Jean?"

"Sandwiches and soup are ready," Jean said, her plump face forming into a forced smile. The morning had been tense and dramatic. Paul and Joanna still weren't perfect. At least not up to Lew Stone's standards, Marisa noted.

She felt sorry for Joanna. She wasn't a strong actress even though she had the right looks and characteristics for the part of Jacqueline. Paul was right for Roland though—conceited, arrogant, handsome. However, he was being pulled down by Joanna's inadequacies. Not that Lew would be the easiest person to work under. Marisa had never actually worked for him. She wasn't particularly looking forward to the next day when she would begin giving her own performance.

She wandered over to the trestle table and ladled

herself out a bowl of soup and took half a ham sandwich from a high-piled plate. When she found a corner, she sat down and began eating. Around her the tense chatter relaxed into friendlier tones. She found herself sipping the soup and relaxing also.

Someone sat down beside her.

"How's it going?" It was Lew.

"Like everyone else." She said. "Tense."

"You haven't done anything yet," he smiled. "I like perfection."

"I noticed," she told him dryly.

"Is it too much to ask?" Again, she noticed how tired he looked. She had to resist the urge to lift her hand and caress his face. She continued to eat her lunch.

"You were up late last night," Lew commented. "I saw your light on past three. Unless you sleep with the light on?"

"I was learning the script," she said. "I haven't had much time."

"I know that, but don't kill yourself over it. I told you to have an early night."

"I want to feel ready for my part. Like you, I aim for perfection."

"Okay," he said, "It's just that Paul and Joanna have had longer to get their acts together."

"I think Paul has," Marisa told him, "but Jo seems very nervous."

"I don't know why. She's an old hand at acting. Would you like some coffee?"

"Please," she nodded and watched as he took their empty soup bowls and got two cups of coffee from Jean. He came back to sit beside her.

"Thank you." She sipped the steaming hot liquid.

Lew stirred milk and sugar in his coffee. "I'm sorry about last night," he said.

"Sorry?" She looked at him in surprise. Lew Stone didn't usually apologize.

"Sorry that I got you mad enough to slam the door in my face."

"You deserved it," she smiled slightly. "And I probably deserved the lecture."

He grinned, "Thanks." It was the first time he'd really smiled at her since they'd met again. It eased the lines of strain on his face. Finishing his coffee, he stood up. "Anyhow, back to work. Now that everyone's got a full stomach, we should get better reactions."

Paul and Joanna were in much better form that afternoon. Although Paul seemed to be carrying her, Joanna gave a passable performance that even Lew couldn't fault. They finished up at six o'clock with quite a bit of usable film.

Supper was much the same as the night before: cold meats and salads set out on tables, beer and soft drinks. Afterward Lew went into conference with some of the crew. They sat around a table beneath a weeping willow having an intense discussion. Lew ran the show, she thought. It was his screenplay, his direction, his production, his money. He called the shots.

Marisa had been summoned to one of the trailers for costume fittings. She went there. Alicia Allen was the costume designer. She was older than Marisa, closer to thirty, tall and very slim, almost boyish, with short cropped black hair and brown eyes. She'd arrived for the first time this afternoon. Lew had stopped what he was doing to go over and speak to her. Later he had shared his coffee break with her. Marisa had seen them both laughing and talking, their heads close together.

The trailer was completely equipped with clothes and sewing machines. Alicia measured Marisa quickly and expertly.

"Lucky you're an off-the-rack size," Alicia said. "There won't be any trouble getting you fixed up."

"That's good," Marisa told her. "I know I was last minute."

"You were?" Alicia arched a black eyebrow, "Lew knew he was going to get you."

"He did?" Marisa said, surprised.

"Lew always gets what he wants," Alicia told her. "You, of all people, should know that."

"Why should I know that, why I hardly know—"

"Oh come on, sweetie." Alicia flicked her tape measure back into its holder. "It was common knowledge in L.A. that you lived with Lew at one time."

Marisa paled, "It was?"

"Of course it was. Don't you know that you were the talk of the town?"

"No," Marisa said truthfully, trying to think back. They'd kept their marriage a secret and she'd never read anything much about the two of them. Of course there had been speculation when they'd been seen together, but they'd avoided interviews. Marisa had always abhorred gossip columns. She never read them. Had Lew known that they were talked about?

"But I know you're married," Alicia's voice broke through Marisa's thoughts.

"How?" Marisa wished she could stop sounding so startled.

"Lew told me, how else?" Alicia smiled knowingly.

"But—" Marisa began. Lew wouldn't do that, would he? Hadn't it been he who had wanted to keep the secret even when Marisa had been bursting to spread her happiness around? Surely, he wouldn't tell Alicia unless they were closer than just casual acquaintances? Was he going to be so cruel as to flaunt a girl friend in front of her? Was Alicia the reason he wanted a divorce?

"Lew and I are old friends." Alicia appeared to read Marisa's thoughts.

Marisa was glad when she had finished her fitting and was able to leave. She walked back to her trailer and got undressed for an early night. Lew was entitled to a girl friend. After all, they had been apart as husband and wife for three years and he was a normal healthy male. Too normal and healthy, Marisa thought wryly, remembering Carla Tomlin.

They hadn't seen much of each other in the first year of their marriage. Lew had been home for only four months before he had to go to Italy to make a film. In those four months together they had managed to get to know each other intimately. With only this short memory of being together Marisa had worked to the peak of her endurance, waiting for the day when Lew would be with her again instead of thousands of miles away. Her only contact with him had been the brief telephone calls that he had made every Sunday evening. She had lived for that moment when she would hear his voice. Until that fatal evening. . . .

It had been a Friday, she remembered bitterly. She had come home late. She had gathered the mail and newspapers on her way in, hoping that the housekeeper had left her a meal. She had been far too tired to prepare anything.

After taking a shower, she had changed into a silk housecoat and collapsed on the velvet couch in the living room. A salad had been left for her. She put it on a tray with a cup of coffee before settling down to read her mail and the papers.

She had only taken a few mouthfuls, put the bills aside, and opened the papers to scan the headlines, when she saw the picture of Lew. But it was not only Lew. In his arms had been Carla Tomlin, the leading lady of his latest film. An American of Italian extraction, she was dark and beautiful, even in the distorted newspaper photograph. Lew was smiling down on her intimately.

Marisa read: *Screenwriter Llewellyn Stone hugs star of his latest film, Carla Tomlin. Miss Tomlin and Mr. Stone have been seen all over Rome together these past few weeks. Miss Tomlin says it's love.*

Marisa had felt as though she were choking. It must be wrong. It must be. Lew wouldn't do that to her. She had reached for the other papers. The story was there too. CARLA'S IN LOVE the headline read.

Her world had seemed in a state of collapse. She had wondered how she would ever get through the weekend—especially Lew's Sunday evening phone call. But that Sunday there had been no call. Out with Carla no doubt. Marisa had buried her despair by washing her hair and taking a bath. She could have gone out with friends. But she did not want to be bombarded by photographers and fans. She did not feel that she had the emotional or physical strength to face them.

Then there had only been a few more days of

shooting on her own film. Somehow she had managed to get through them. Luckily most of the more dramatic and complicated work had been filmed earlier. Lew was due home in two weeks.

By the time he arrived back in California the story of his involvement with Carla Tomlin had appeared in all the movie magazines.

Mark Lawson had picked him up from the airport assuming that Marisa would be busy with her own work, but Marisa had been home. Though it had been over three years ago, the details of that terrible meeting were etched on Marisa's memory.

She had been in the kitchen when she heard the key turn in the lock. Her heart gave a sickening lurch. All the words that she had thought to say had suddenly vanished.

"Mari!" Lew called. She heard him go through the house and come into the kitchen. "Sweetheart, how are you?" He approached her and embraced her with all his strength, his mouth claiming hers. "Ah, how I have missed you," he whispered huskily. He held her a little away, "Missed me?"

"Of course," she had told him, lowering her eyes. "Would you like a drink?"

He stared at her, his arms still linked around her waist, "Is that all you're going to offer, or, do I have a choice?" There was an edge to his smile.

She had pulled away and busied herself pouring a Scotch for him and a sherry for herself. She handed him his drink.

His glance had taken in her movements. "What's the matter with you?" he asked. "You seem so tense."

"I've just been working hard," she said evasively. "How was your flight home?"

"Like all flights," he answered irritably. He finished his whisky at a gulp. Stretching and unbuttoning his shirt, he walked toward the bedroom. "I'm going to take a shower, and get changed. Care to join me?" he asked. His tone was mocking.

"No—I—I have to see what is going on in the kitchen." She refused to look at him.

"Whatever you wish," he muttered, striding through the house to the bedroom and closing the door behind him. Marisa heard him taking off his clothes—the thump of his boots as they hit the floor, the rattle of his belt buckle on the chair, but she was determined to block out of her mind his lean naked body tanned dark by the Italian sun.

She had been setting the table when he had come up noiselessly behind her. He was not yet fully dressed. Above his brief, denim shorts droplets of water still clung to the smoothness of his tanned shoulders. He pulled Marisa back against him with a strong arm and she felt his lips travel against her neck and down to her shoulder. She took a deep breath to stop the weak feeling that always seemed to come from his touch.

"Is supper ready?" he murmured, his lips against her skin, his hand moving to cup the fullness of her breast.

"It's ready," she said unsteadily. "I think we'd better eat."

He stopped fondling her and let her go abruptly. "Yes, let's eat. It's obvious that you don't feel inclined to let me make love with you."

"I'm tired Lew," she lied.

"Of course you are. So am I. But that doesn't mean that I don't want to make love with my wife, especially after being so far away from her."

"You have had other diversions," she told him.

His eyes narrowed. "What do you mean by that?" he asked.

"Carla Tomlin," she said coolly. "It's all over town."

"Is it?" He raised an eyebrow.

"What did you expect? That I'd sit home here ignorant of the fact that you were—" she gestured vaguely, "out over there with that woman—"

"I don't deny that she was there." His eyes were like chips of ice.

"You probably can't deny anything," Marisa flung at him.

Lew laughed harshly. "Oh, I could probably find a few things to deny. The media has been known to exaggerate, you know." He walked over to the table. "Why don't we eat now and talk later," he said. "Your steaks will be ruined."

"I suppose," Lew said when he'd finished eating and was pouring himself another full glass of wine, "that this has been brewing in your mind for days now."

"Am I supposed to ignore it?" Marisa asked.

He swirled the wine around in his glass. "I did come home expecting to get greeted by a warm loving wife, not a snarling witch."

"Then will you deny you were with Carla?" She held her breath.

He got up from the table abruptly, "How can I deny I was with Carla, when I was with Carla? How can I deny that?"

"I know she was in Italy with you, but can you deny the rumors?"

"And if I do?" he asked silkily. "Will you believe me?"

"I *might*," she told him.

"Then what's the point?" he said, angrily turning away from her. "What the hell's the point?"

She watched his broad back, the tenseness of the muscles across his shoulders, the slim hips and long legs also showing tension.

"You never called on Sunday," Marisa said bleakly, adding the other thing that had been on her mind.

"No I didn't." He turned around again. "I got tied up in a meeting and it was too late, you would have been in bed."

"There was Monday—"

"I was busy Marisa," he snapped at her.

"But not too busy for Carla."

"Damn!" He turned away again.

"She was a friend of yours before we were married," Marisa said.

"Yes." He still had his back to her.

"I suppose that means that you were—"

"Maybe we were," he yelled, whipping around again. "You're not the first one in my life. I am thirty-five you know, I wasn't hanging around saving myself for you."

"I didn't expect—" she began.

His eyes flashed dangerously, "I don't know what to expect from your puritanical Victorian mind. I thought since we'd been married you'd improved, but you haven't. You're still cool and insensitive. I don't know why I bothered. I should have just taken you to bed and to hell with the consequences."

He moved toward the table and put down the empty wineglass. Then he turned his back and went toward the bedroom.

"Where're you going?" She followed him to the bedroom door and watched as he took off the shorts and started to dress in jeans and a denim shirt.

"To seek out some company that is pleasant to be with," he told her, checking to make sure that he had his wallet and keys with him.

He pushed past her at the bedroom door and went toward the front door.

"Carla came home on the flight with me," he told her. "So she's in town. Don't wait up."

Then the door slammed shut and Marisa had never felt so alone in all her life.

It had been a long night. Marisa had undressed and gone to bed, but she hadn't been able to sleep, and then, when she did, it was to wake up to a brilliant sunshine, but no Lew. He'd stayed out all night. With Carla? He hadn't denied anything about their affair, and he had implied that they'd been lovers before he'd married Marisa.

The day had been interminable. It lengthened into evening and still she hadn't heard from Lew. Finally Marisa could stand it no longer. She had phoned Mark Lawson. He had told her that he had not heard from Lew all day. She thought she detected a note of pity in his voice.

Leave, an inner voice had said to her. *Leave before he can come back and hurt you more. He may like having a sweet, innocent wife at home, but it will never satisfy him. He needs an experienced, older woman— like Carla Tomlin.*

Without even informing Mark, she left for Canada that afternoon. To this day she had no recollection of packing her belongings and the taxi ride to the airport. Only the picture of Carla Tomlin and Lew was indelibly imprinted in her mind.

And nothing has changed, she thought, restlessly tossing in her trailer bed. The script has not changed, only the actors. Three years ago it had been Carla and Lew, now it was Alicia and Lew. From the bottom of her heart Marisa wished that she had had the courage to refuse to sign the contract for "The Rain Lady."

Chapter Ten

It poured the next day. They'd started early in a watery
sun, but by nine o'clock the thunder clouds had rolled
in and lightning flashed across the fields. They all
moved into the house. The workmen were banging in
the hallway, but the kitchen had been painted and
cleaned and was usable.

Jean made coffee and served it with small cakes and
cookies. Everyone sat around the big kitchen table.
Lew didn't join them, however, and neither, Marisa
noticed, did Alicia Allen.

Marisa felt rather headachy and depressed. She
blamed a restless night and the heaviness of the
weather. In a way she was glad it had rained them out.
She wouldn't have been much good as Marion today.
Feeling slightly sick after the cup of coffee, she got up
and decided to look over the house. The windows

weren't shuttered anymore and the light, such as it was, streamed through from outside. The floors were all solid wood. They only needed a good polish to get them shiny again. The rooms were large and well proportioned.

She went upstairs and peered into some of them. There was furniture, but most of it was covered by ghostly dust sheets. Then she came to a section of the house that looked lived in, and, curiously, she looked into the first room. It was a bedroom. The walls had been painted an off-white. The bed was low and of Scandinavian design covered with a brown and beige duvet. The curtains were the same design as the bed cover.

The carpet was off-white, thick and springy. She walked in further and saw that a door at the other end of the room was open revealing a bathroom tiled in the same shades as the bedroom. A leather shaving kit stood open on the window ledge with Lew's initials scrolled in gold upon it. Marisa felt a lump form in her throat. She'd given him that shaving kit for his birthday a few weeks after their marriage. So this was Lew's room. He was living in the house.

She went back into the bedroom. The closet door was partly open and she could see a shirt hung carelessly on a hanger. Touching the cuff tentatively, she felt tears well in her eyes.

"Okay, what are you doing?"

Marisa jumped in surprise, pulling the shirt off its hanger as she did so.

"I'm sorry," she said, fumbling with the shirt and the wire hanger and trying to push it back into the closet.

"Let me," Lew said, taking the garment from her and securing it on the rail. Then he closed the closet door.

His eyes were cool. "What are you trying to do? Get some evidence against me? Maybe a trace of lipstick, a long blond hair?"

"I—I was just curious," she stammered, "I didn't know you were living up here."

"You never asked," he said. He was wearing jeans and a shirt, open halfway down his chest exposing the "love" medallion.

"Actually I was looking for you," he said. "I was wondering if you needed anything in Parkville, the neighboring town. I'm driving Alicia in."

Marisa shook her head, "No I don't need anything." Even if she did, she wouldn't go with him and Alicia. Let him carry on his affairs without involving her.

"You're not just saying that because of Alicia?" he asked, as if he'd read her thoughts.

"Why should she bother me?"

"I wouldn't know," he said innocently. "But I am entitled to girl friends you know, even though you and I are still married. An absentee wife doesn't do much for a man's sex life."

"I don't care whom you sleep with," Marisa told him, hoping she sounded calm, though her heart was beating fast.

"Don't you?" he asked, looking into her eyes. His weren't so icy now, but dark as though his emotions had been aroused. Maybe they had been, by Alicia.

"No." Marisa turned away from the disturbing influence of his gaze.

"No I guess not. You're cool, very cool. You always

were. I guess that's your mystery. Your poise." He turned and went to the door. "The rain has stopped by the way," he said. "But I'm giving everyone the rest of the day off."

Marisa stayed in Lew's bedroom for a few minutes after he'd left, regaining the poise Lew claimed she possessed. She had been brought up strictly. To be seen and not heard. To hide her emotions. Once she'd dared drag those emotions out and in return she'd been desperately hurt.

Marisa had been in bed for hours when she heard the sound of a car in the driveway and footsteps outside the trailers.

Alicia's voice was loud. "Thank you for a lovely day, darling," she said.

Lew said something, quiet and indistinguishable. Then there was a long silence. Probably a kiss. Then the door of a trailer closed. Marisa held her breath. Footsteps sounded across the grass toward the house. Lew was going home to his own bed. Then Marisa slept.

The week ran into the weekend. Sunday was a day off. Most of the crew went into Toronto to visit friends, or just to break the monotony. Lew went off in his car on Saturday night with an exuberant Alicia by his side.

Marisa slept late on Sunday. She pottered around the trailer preparing coffee. The whole site seemed to be deserted and silent. Not that it bothered her. It was nice to be able to have a day to take things easy and sort out her thoughts. Of course she could have gone home to her apartment. She probably would next weekend, but the thought of the drive down to Toronto seemed exhausting at the moment. Besides, there was no one there, other than John, whom she cared to see.

The phone was hooked up inside Lew's house now. She would phone John later and let him know the number, but right now she was going to go for a walk. She didn't get to the country often. It all looked so green and fresh that she could hardly wait to get outside into the sunshine.

She dressed in a pair of cream denim jeans, a yellow shirt and sandals, and perched a pair of sunglasses on her nose. She was about to set off along a mysterious looking path that wound its way through a clump of woods and across the fields, when Paul Dexter intercepted.

"Going somewhere?" he asked. He was dressed casually in blue jeans with a black T-shirt that hugged his chest muscles.

"I was going for a walk. I thought I was the only one here today."

"I thought I'd stick around," Paul told her, his dark eyes obviously admiring her. "May I join you?"

"I suppose so," Marisa told him. She didn't really have much choice.

"Don't sound so enthusiastic," he said, as they started off along the dirt track, now dry after the rain earlier that week.

"I'm sorry Paul," she said. "It's just that I feel rather tired and I might not be much of a companion."

"I think you're a gorgeous companion," Paul smiled at her, "and a great actress."

"Why thank you." Marisa was flattered.

"Lew Stone thinks you're pretty good too."

"Did he tell you that?" Marisa asked, before she could stop herself.

"As a matter of fact, he did. The other night when we were having a chat."

Marisa pushed back a branch and held it for Paul to duck under. She really had no qualms about what Lew thought of her acting, just as she had no doubts about his writing, or directing ability. It was their personal relationship that was uncertain.

"You knew him before, didn't you?" Paul said.

Marisa was in front of him and murmured an affirmation. She didn't want to get into a discussion about Lew with Paul Dexter.

"Well?" Paul asked.

"Professionally," Marisa said, "like now."

"From what I heard it was more," Paul said.

"I guess your source was wrong. You know how newspapers are."

"This was Alicia Allen," Paul said.

"I hardly know Alicia," Marisa said, wanting the conversation to end.

"She knows Lew well," Paul persisted.

"Lew knows a lot of women well," Marisa told him cynically.

"But not you?"

"No," Marisa said. Paul edged closer to her.

"Then you're free?" Paul asked.

"It all depends what you mean by free," she said lightly.

"Well I mean here we are, two perfectly healthy, beautiful people, alone on a Sunday afternoon with an entire evening ahead of us."

"Paul," she chided, taking a step backward.

"Will you come for dinner with me then? There's a place in Parkville that's passable."

Marisa gave in to that. She didn't fancy an evening sitting around wondering what Lew and Alicia were doing.

They completed their walk, finding that the path wound in a complete circle out of the woods and then across the fields back toward the house. Paul seemed pleased that he'd made a date with her. After all, he was a handsome man, Marisa told herself, and famous, as well as her leading man. Why not be seen around with him?

Dinner turned out to be very enjoyable. Paul's choice was a country restaurant patronized by a lot of city dwellers looking for a change of scene. The meal was delicious and Paul was an entertaining companion. Marisa, whose male contacts had been limited over the past three years, enjoyed the experience of being with an attractive flirtatious man again.

They drove back in Paul's Mercedes. Both felt as though they had had a good time.

At the door to her trailer Paul kissed her lightly.

"Thank you Marisa," he said. "I had a wonderful time."

"You sound surprised." She smiled.

"I thought you might be a bit dull," he admitted. "You've seemed so quiet around the set."

"When I'm working, I work hard."

"And play hard?" Paul raised a dark eyebrow.

"It depends," she told him cautiously, realizing what she could get herself into if she said too much.

"More like hard to get," Paul said, and they both

laughed. Paul squeezed her arm and left her. She watched him walk up the steps to his trailer, turn on the light and close the door. She sighed contentedly. It had been a good evening. Paul, surprisingly, hadn't become physically demanding.

She went up the steps, and opened the door, but before she could grope for the light switch, Lew's voice said, "Don't turn on the light."

"What are you doing in here?" she asked, her voice shaking. His large form moved out of one of the armchairs.

"I was waiting for you. It's past midnight."

"I'm quite aware of that," she said.

"Been out with Dexter?"

"Yes, but it's none of your business."

"I'm your husband."

"In name only," she said, her eyes becoming accustomed to the darkness.

The dress she had chosen for the evening was pencil slim with spaghetti straps and a plain bodice. It was a very pale blue but looked silver in the darkness. She moved to place the shawl she had been holding over the back of an armchair. Lew must have moved too, because when she straightened from where she had flung the shawl, he was standing right in front of her.

"Paul Dexter's married," he said. "Did he mention it?"

"He didn't," she told him. "But then it doesn't matter."

"Why? Because you're married too? So it's all fair?"

"I didn't mean that," she said. "Look, Lew, I'm tired. Would you please leave."

"I was hoping that I might be offered coffee," he

suggested lightly, as though it were natural for him to be creeping around her trailer at night.

"Fine," Marisa said, "I'll need a light though."

Lew pushed the switch on a small light over the table. He stood beside her as she prepared the coffee. The dull lighting softened the harsher lines of his features, making his lips more vulnerable and the lines of strain less evident. Marisa felt her heart turn over slightly. She'd been with him many times such as this during their brief marriage.

"Did you have a nice day with Alicia?" she asked.

"Yes," he said, taking the coffee cup she offered. She sipped her own. She didn't want to sit down. Sitting might relax her, and she knew, she was vulnerable, even though she had thought herself cured of the attraction she felt toward him.

"Where did you go?" she asked conversationally.

"We went up to the top of the CN Tower to eat dinner and see the view," he said. "As if you were interested."

"Oh but I am," she told him with forced brightness. The thought of him with Alicia gave her a jealous stab.

"What else do you want to know then?" he asked.

She wanted to say *Did you make love to her? Did she make your heart beat fast with her kisses and her touch?*

"That's all," she said.

His eyes held hers, "And what did you do with Dexter?"

"We went for dinner in Parkville. It was pleasant."

"Pleasant," he growled, putting the empty cup on the table with a thump. "Do you still see life in those pallid words. Isn't there any emotion in your world? No quickening heartbeats, no passion—" He drew her into his arms, his lips moving against the hollow of her throat, drawing back the narrow strap of her gown so that she could feel his teeth against her soft skin.

"Don't," she murmured.

"Why? Because it disturbs your placid existence? I can never understand how you can be such a good actress. You are so cold." She felt the zipper move at the back of her dress and his hand came around to caress the soft skin beneath. "But you're not really cold are you, Marisa? Your heart is beating now."

She was reaching up to him, her fingers in his unruly hair, her lips seeking his, but he pushed her away.

"So Dexter didn't get his way tonight," he snapped. "I was wondering if you would let him."

"Get out!" she cried, holding up the front of her dress. "Just get out. You've got no right."

"No rights?" He arched an eyebrow. "I think I have rights where you are concerned, my *wife.*"

Then he moved away from her. She heard the door slam and his footsteps moving away toward the big house.

Marisa undressed slowly and then huddled beneath the covers in the bed. It was a hot night but she was shivering violently. She tossed and turned for hours. Finally, as light began to filter through the little trailer windows, she fell into a restless sleep.

Chapter Eleven

On Monday morning the entire crew packed up their gear and went into Parkville. It was an attractive little Ontario town. Orange brick buildings lined the main street. On the side streets, huge, old mansions with white painted porches were surrounded by large old trees. As they filmed, they attracted a crowd. Marisa found that it was more like acting in a stage play than a film. It probably helped to have an audience. She needed to be distracted after her encounter with Lew the night before.

Toni, who did the makeup, commented on her looks.

"You need more makeup today," she said, putting on foundation with a heavy hand. "Not sleeping well?"

"It must be the change of surroundings," Marisa told her.

"Probably Lew's slave-driving more like it," Toni said, applying eye shadow. "Joanna looks almost haggard."

Marisa didn't answer, but sat quietly through the remainder of the makeup session. She didn't want to discuss Lew with anyone. She just wanted to get this whole thing over with, then get her divorce and be completely free.

Now that the film crew had shown up in Parkville, the press, radio and television stations had caught up with them. Lew pulled Marisa aside during a break.

"We're signed on for a television talk show tomorrow night," he told her. "We have to go down and tape it in the afternoon."

"We?"

"You and I."

"Not Paul?" She didn't want to travel to Toronto alone with Lew, or be subjected to scrutiny across the country with him beside her on a television show.

"Paul's doing his piece now." Lew indicated Paul giving a television station an on-the-set interview.

"But I don't want to go with you," she whispered.

"Marisa." His fingers dug into her arm. "We need the publicity. I'm putting quite a bit of my own money into this thing. I don't want to see it bust."

She tried to release her arm but his hold was too tight. She would only attract attention if she struggled.

"Well, do you want to see me broke?" he demanded. "Do you?"

"Of course not," she muttered.

"Then you'll do the interview with me?"

"Do I have a choice?" She eyed him defiantly. After the way he'd made a fool of her last night in her trailer, she really had no desire to please him.

"Not really," he told her, and let go of her arm abruptly, as though her flesh were distasteful to him.

"The interview's at two tomorrow," he said. "We'll go in for lunch."

Marisa opened her mouth to object, but closed it when she saw his ice-cold expression. No one argued with Lew Stone when he looked like that.

The next day was warm and windy. As Lew would be away, the crew packed up at noon. Marisa went to her trailer to change. She chose to wear a dress with a simple collarless neckline, the blue cotton material reflecting the blue of her eyes. She slipped a silver chain around her neck. Pleased with her appearance, she met Lew outside the house beside his car.

He was dressed in a denim suit and a pale blue shirt that emphasized his dark tan. The medallion at his throat glinted in the sunlight.

"Both in blue," he commented, as he opened her side of the car.

"I—I tried for something simple for television," she told him, settling into the low seat of the Porsche. He got in beside her and started the engine.

"You look fine," he said indifferently.

They drove down the driveway and out on to the highway. The fast car ate up the miles. Marisa was glad for his silence. She kept her gaze riveted on the fields and farmhouses they passed.

"Any preference where you would like to eat lunch?" he asked, as they stopped for a red light.

Marisa shook her head. "Anywhere," she told him dully.

"What the hell is wrong with you?" he asked, swearing at the quick shift of gears as the light turned green.

"I don't know what you mean," she said stiffly.

"Oh come on," he sighed. "You're strung up like a tightrope."

"Because you're domineering and boorish, and I don't like your company."

He accelerated the car through an orange light that turned to red midway, just missing a turning car.

"What the hell do you mean by that?" he shouted.

"Just what it sounds like," she told him, getting angry herself. "Sunday night you came into my trailer and threw all sorts of accusations at me. You've no right."

"We're still married, Marisa," he reminded her, more controlled now.

"In my book we haven't been married for three years," she said.

"Well in my book, we're still married, sweetheart."

"Oh why did you have to come back?" she sighed, turning to look blindly out of the car window.

"Did you think you could just disappear out of my life forever? What if I wanted another wife, maybe children?"

She turned back to him, "I didn't think of that."

"No, you didn't. You never think of anyone but your precious self."

"That's not true," she told him.

"Then prove it," he said, glancing at her.

"How?" she asked.

"By behaving as though you want to be with me."

"But I don't."

"Act, Marisa. That is your profession. This afternoon on that show you're going to have to look as though you enjoy my company, so you might as well get used to it now."

Lunch was a quiet, polite affair in a seafood restaurant overlooking Lake Ontario and the Toronto islands. Marisa talked to Lew when she had to, but at other times, watched the ferry wind its way across the blue waters of the lake.

After lunch, Lew drove directly to the television studio. They were made up and Paul Ryan, their host, talked to them beforehand as a warm-up. Then they were both before the camera, Paul Ryan relaxed and casual in a brown safari suit and cream shirt and brown tie, Marisa and Lew sitting together on a love seat beside him.

Paul started by asking a number of technical questions which Lew answered easily. Lew sat with his right leg propped up over his left thigh. Marisa sat mesmerized, watching his foot in its expensive leather boot.

"And, Marisa," Paul Ryan asked, "how does it feel to be back in the movies?"

"Marvelous," Marisa shrugged. She saw Lew's mouth twist cynically. She smiled brightly. "It's all very exciting. I—I missed acting very much. I didn't know how much until this great opportunity."

"Then why did you stay away for so long?" Paul Ryan glanced inconspicuously at his notes.

"Oh," Marisa smiled again, "I felt that I needed a rest. Contrary to popular opinion, acting is hard work."

"Was your husband against your acting?" Paul Ryan asked. Marisa stared at him, stunned.

"My—my husband?"

"Lew here," Paul nodded toward Lew. "Did he want you to act? To have a career of your own?"

Realizing that she couldn't deny their marriage on television without creating a scandal, she said, "No. No, it wasn't anything to do with him." She glanced at Lew and saw that his lips were curved with amusement.

"And am I to understand that you were here in Toronto the whole time and we didn't know it?" Paul Ryan asked, excited that he'd opened up a whole new area—the Lew Stone-Marisa Marshall relationship.

"Yes I was here," Marisa said. "It's my home you know."

"Oh I know that, and Lew's too. Probably when you two met down in California, that was something you had in common, and bound you together. I understand Lew Stone got you your first chance in the movies?"

"Sort of," Marisa told him, annoyed at Paul Ryan for being so outspoken, and at Lew for allowing it to go on.

Lew broke in on the conversation. "Marisa got by on her own talent," he said quietly. "Granted, I put in a word for her, but you have to prove yourself even if you do have the right connections. I think Marisa proved herself, and will again in 'The Rain Lady.' We did come here to discuss 'The Rain Lady,' didn't we?"

Paul Ryan flushed beneath Lew's glance.

"It's true we're married," Lew went on, "we married secretly in the hope of getting some privacy. But I don't think anything can be kept private in this business." Lew smiled to soften his words. His hand reached for Marisa's and gave it a reassuring squeeze. "It's good to be working with her," he added.

Paul Ryan beamed at them both and then went on to

ask both of them noncommittal questions about "The Rain Lady" until the interview finally ended.

Out in the bright sunshine of the parking lot, Marisa leaned against the Porsche.

"Too much for you?" Lew asked. She noticed that he too looked strained. His face was pale beneath the tan.

Marisa inhaled deeply trying to fend off dizziness.

"Are you okay?" Lew's arm came around her shoulders.

She nodded, and leaned against him.

"Oh, honey." Lew stroked the curls back from her forehead. "I know it got a little embarrassing at times, but it was fine. They'll edit out anything that seemed too stilted."

"He'll leave everything in," Marisa said wearily. "He had a piece of gossip and he used it."

"Does it matter?" Lew asked.

"Does what matter?" She glanced up at him.

"That everyone knows we're married?"

She shook her head. "I suppose not."

"Of course it doesn't." He continued to stroke her hair. She noticed a pulse beating erratically in his cheek.

"But you'll have to tell the crew that we're getting a divorce," Marisa told him.

"We *could* do that," he said.

"We *have to*, Lew," she said firmly.

He looked at her suspiciously. "I guess you don't want your boy friends thinking you're tied up with me. Is that it?" he asked, letting his arm drop from her shoulders. Despite the warmth of the day, she felt chilly without his support.

"That's it," she told him, knowing it was a lie. She had no boyfriends. No one else had ever meant anything to her. *Or ever would,* she thought helplessly.

"Okay I'll let everyone know, but you must do your bit too. Why don't you tell Dexter? He'll get it around quickly enough."

"Then you'll tell Alicia?" Marisa asked. They eyed each other coldly over the top of the low car.

"I'll tell Alicia, don't worry," he said.

The next evening Marisa phoned John Benton. She tried to keep the conversation light and friendly.

"The filming is going smoothly," she said, answering John's immediate questions. The phone had been installed in the study inside the house and she was seated at the desk. She noticed, as she talked, that the drawers of the desk were filled with papers. An expensive, streamlined, electric typewriter sat on a side table. There was a huge, brick fireplace and Marisa imagined a cozy, blazing fire with the snow piled high outside.

"Is it possible for me to come up and see you?" John asked.

"Of course. I was going to go home on the weekend, but if you want, come up here instead."

"I'll come up Sunday," John told her. "I'd love a day in the country."

"It's beautiful and peaceful up here, John."

"How's it going with Lew?" he asked.

"Fine," she told him noncommittally.

"That's good. No problems?"

She knew what he meant, but said, "No. None at all."

"Good. I saw that interview on television and wondered."

She'd also watched the interview and as Lew had told her, there had been some editing. Actually it hadn't come off too badly in spite of the tense moment when Paul Ryan was soliciting his juicy piece of gossip.

"I don't think it did either of you any harm. I was wondering at first, but to see you both together. Well, you're a handsome couple. People will love you."

"That's good," Marisa murmured. She heard the door click and looked up and saw Lew standing on the threshold. They hadn't spoken on their trip back up north last night and the day had been filled with hard work.

John was saying, "So it's Sunday then, sweetheart. I'm looking forward to seeing you. I miss you."

"I miss you too," she said. "See you then." She hung up.

Lew closed the door behind him.

"Sorry to butt in," he said.

"It was only John," she told him, getting up from the chair behind the desk.

"Only?" he queried.

"He is my agent," she said, moving toward the door to leave, but he held her arm.

"You look tired," he said. She was surprised.

"I've been working hard." She tried to smile, but it was hard to smile when he was so close.

"Tell me if it gets too much for you?"

"I can handle it, don't worry."

His fingers moved sensuously against her bare arm.

"I'm not worried," he told her, "I just don't want you overdoing things."

"I won't, I promise you," she said.

His eyes probed hers, "The interview's still bothering you?"

"Not really," she shook her head. She'd been subjected to a few curious stares, but everyone was being tactful.

"Most of these people I've known for a long time," Lew said. "They won't hurt you."

"Only you can do that," she said, and then wished she hadn't, as his fingers dug into her arm.

"Physically, yes," he said.

"Let me go!" She tried to pull away from him, her blue eyes mutinous beneath his icy gray stare.

"And if I don't?" His nails scratched the surface of her smooth flesh.

"Then I'll have to find some way of hurting you," she spat out.

"That, you've already done," he said, abruptly letting go of her arm. He moved toward his desk, and opened a carved wooden box to take a slim cigar. He put the cigar between his lips and lit it with his lighter. "Now please go Marisa, I've got some work to do."

"With pleasure," she retorted, disturbed to feel tears filling her eyes as she slammed out of his office. Later, when she stared from her trailer window, the light in his study was still shining. It was almost four in the morning.

Chapter Twelve

From then on they worked hard, packing up at dusk and beginning again at six the next morning. Sometimes Marisa wondered how she would manage the stamina to keep going. But she wanted the hard work; it made it that much easier to forget Lew and her memories.

There was a party on Saturday evening for the crew and the press. Marisa had a hard time trying to decide what to wear. Finally she chose a calf-length skirt in printed cherry silk and a paler silk long-sleeved blouse. She could wear the blouse buttoned low with a varied number of necklaces and add a pair of high-heeled sandals to give it a dress-up look. She didn't look bad, she thought, as she swirled in front of the full-length mirror that was attached to the trailer closet door, except that her face looked rather pinched and tired. Clever makeup would eliminate that problem. When she slipped beside Paul Dexter into his Mercedes, she felt at ease with herself.

The Parkville Hotel was possibly in the exact condition as when it was first built in the early nineteen hundreds; it had been renovated to look as much like the original as possible. The rooms that had been reserved for the dinner and party were joined by a short hallway. One room was set with tables, and the other cleared for dancing, with an orchestra set up in one corner. The floors were highly polished dark wood. Crystal chandeliers hung from the ceilings. Some of the windows were stained glass.

They were served an excellent dinner. Marisa sat next to a reporter, with Paul Dexter on her other side. She had to deal with both, but she still managed to eat all the iced melon and a delicious sole cooked in a white wine sauce. Lew was a gracious host, sitting at the head of the table, making sure each person had his share of service, food and publicity.

Alicia sat beside Lew. She was wearing a silky, low-cut orange dress that did wonders for her California tanned skin and black hair. Lew's smile, it seemed to Marisa, was warmer than she'd ever seen it, when he directed his glance toward Alicia, and Alicia was obviously radiant.

After the meal came dancing. Although Marisa did not lack partners, she stayed with Paul. He was a handsome, compelling partner, as proficient at dancing as he was at acting. A good escort, he made sure that Marisa always had a drink in hand, a smile on her face, and was never kept standing about awkwardly.

But after a while even this lavish attention palled. When Paul took a moment to dance with Joanna

Mason, Marisa managed to skip out the back way to the terrace that led down to a tiny stream where the water cascaded in silver brightness.

She stood watching the stream skip over the stones, wondering what it was about water that was so compelling. She felt clear headed tonight even though she'd had quite a bit to drink. Perhaps it was exhilaration at being noticed again—having someone interested enough to print her story, her thoughts, even her face, on the front of a newspaper. She smiled to herself, brushing a silvery lock of hair away from her cheek.

"Penny for them," a voice said behind her.

"Do you have to keep creeping up on me?" she said lightly. She wasn't going to let Lew Stone's presence bother her tonight. Tonight was hers.

"I guess we just seem to travel in the same directions," he answered in the same light tone. He paused to take one of his small cigars from a gold case and lit it with his gold lighter. Then he put the case and lighter away. "Are you happy, now that you're in the limelight again?"

"Yes," she told him honestly. "Who wouldn't be?"

"Someone who has hidden away from it for three years."

"I was never scared of the limelight."

"Then what were you scared of?" He puffed on the cigar and blew smoke into rings.

"Not the limelight," she faltered, realizing that he'd almost trapped her. He looked rather formidable out here in the darkness, dressed in his formal black suit. The effect was somewhat softened by his ruffled shirt and the velvet necktie, carelessly undone.

"Then what?" he asked.

"I was ill."

He turned toward her. "Ill?"

"You know how it is in this business."

"I know, but I never thought you'd go that way."

"Why should I be different?"

"I—" He threw the half smoked cigar into the small stream. "I thought you had the strength," he said.

"Well I didn't, I buckled."

"You seem to have recovered now." It was more a statement than a question.

She nodded, "It's surprising what a rest can do."

"I'm sure." The tone was ironic. "They seem to be ensconced in the hotel for the night," he said after a pause, glancing back. "I think I'll make my way home. Would you like a lift?"

"I came with Paul," she said.

"As you like," he shrugged his shoulders, pulling further on the velvet necktie so that it came completely loose. He stuffed it in his pocket.

"Didn't you accompany Alicia Allen?" she asked.

"I didn't plan to abandon her," he said dryly, "I only offered you a *lift*."

"Then I'm sure you'd rather be alone with her," she said sweetly. Not even Lew Stone was going to upset her this evening. She swept past him and back into the hotel to seek out Paul.

Chapter Thirteen

There was a light knocking on her door. Marisa turned over in the narrow bunk bed and looked at her clock. It read almost noon. With a groan, she got up and slipped on a robe and went to open her door. It was John Benton.

"Hi sweetheart," he said smiling, looking fresh and wide awake.

"Oh John," she said. "Come on in. We had a party last night and I must have overslept." She put out her hand, glad to see a friendly face. Someone she didn't have to act for.

John came up the steps and into the trailer. "I hung around for a while outside," he said. "Then I saw Lew Stone and a gorgeous woman getting into his car. He told me what trailer you were staying in."

"That's nice of him," Marisa said, thinking that the

gorgeous woman was probably Alicia. "Do you want some coffee?"

"Please." John sat down at the little table. "This is a nice trailer you have. Star treatment?"

"Something like that." Marisa smiled and went over to the stove to prepare the coffee. "Well, how's business?" she asked.

"Much better," John told her. "Of course having you on my list brings others my way."

"I'm glad." She put out two mugs. "Have you had breakfast?"

"I did have something." He looked around him. "This is a great place. I hear Lew Stone owns the house."

"Apparently, yes," Marisa said.

"I wonder what he wants it for? L.A. seems more his style." John shook his head in amazement.

"Who can tell what Lew's style is?" Marisa handed John his coffee and sat opposite.

"You're right," John agreed. "He just seems more L.A. to me."

"Lew is his own man," Marisa told him. "He could exist anywhere."

"Probably," John grinned. "How's the filming going?"

"Not bad. A few hitches but it's to be expected. We seem to be pretty much on schedule."

"Good." John stared down into his coffee cup. He seemed edgy this morning, Marisa thought.

"Is there anything bothering you, John?" Marisa asked after he'd stared at his coffee in silence for more than five minutes.

"No." He looked up startled, and then stood up and walked to the trailer window. "Marisa," he said, "Clara and I are getting back together."

"You're what?"

"Clara and I have decided to get back together," he said. "I was over there this morning having breakfast."

"Are you sure, John?"

"Of course, I'm sure. We've talked it over for some time now. We think it's best for us, and for the kids."

"Oh I'm glad. Really I am," Marisa told him.

"So," he looked down at the table, "That offer I made you—"

"Forget it," she told him. "I'm just happy for you that it's worked out again with Clara."

"I just wish it could be the same for you and Lew."

She shook her head. "No. Lew and I never had the long-term relationship that you had with Clara. It was brief and passionate, but that was all. Nothing lasting."

"If you say so," he said.

"I say so. Now let me get dressed, and I'll show you around this place."

They spent a pleasant afternoon around the grounds of the house and then went for a leisurely walk across the fields. John took Marisa out for an early dinner before he drove home.

After he'd gone, she sat on the steps of her trailer. It was quiet now, before everyone started arriving back for work tomorrow morning. Maybe she would go home next weekend. Just to check up on her mail and apartment.

It was close to ten o'clock when she heard the sound of a powerful engine. Lew's car. She hurried into her trailer and closed the door. She didn't want to see Lew that night.

The work week went well. Joanna improved and Paul was as good as usual. Marisa was able to hold her end up. They ended on Friday with quite a bit of usable footage.

Marisa had decided to go down to Toronto for the weekend. She'd go early Saturday morning and probably come back Sunday morning. That would give her Sunday afternoon in the country which she was enjoying so much.

Her apartment seemed just the same. She did a load of wash in the small washing machine in the bathroom, vacuumed the floors and checked the mail. There was quite a bit. A film offer in California. She'd have to sit down and consider that one. Maybe she was off to the big time again. The thought scared and excited her.

She changed her wardrobe, taking another evening dress with her in case there was another party as there inevitably would be.

Parties on the set during filming seemed to be necessary to release the tension that was built up.

She didn't call John. He was probably with Clara and his children anyhow and didn't need her around. No one really needed her anymore, she thought. Lew had never needed her, not in the spiritual sense that she'd needed him. When bored with her physically, he had strayed to greener pastures.

She decided that she'd drive back up north that evening instead of the next day. It was raining when she left the freeway and started off on the narrower

two-laned road that led toward Parkville. And as the
rain got heavier it seemed to Marisa that it was flooding
the road. The car windows were steamed up and the
rain was pounding hard against the windshield. There
was no visibility beyond the faint flash of the car's
headlights.

Then the car slowed down of its own accord and no
amount of pushing on the gas pedal revived it. The
engine died. Slipping the gearshift back into neutral,
Marisa tried to start it, but it was no good.

"Damn," she muttered to herself. Probably she
would have to sit here until the rain stopped, and that
could be all night. Then, she realized that she would
have to get the car off the road or another car could
come along and smash into her.

She got out of the car. The wind lashed at her hair
and clothes. Within seconds, the rain had drenched
her. Using all her strength, she pushed the car to the
shoulder of the road. That would have to do, she
thought, *I have no more strength.*

She got back inside the car and tried to start it once
more, but the engine was completely dead.

Well, she couldn't sit here all night! She didn't think
she was far from the trailer site. She'd have to walk.
With any luck the rain would ease slightly.

She had a zippered windbreaker in the car and she
put that on over her sodden clothing. She locked the
car, then clutching her purse beneath the windbreaker,
began to walk.

The rain eased for a few minutes, though the wind
was still gusting. But the relief was only temporary. A
flash of lightning, followed by a roll of thunder,

preceded a torrential downpour. Marisa struggled along the pitch-black, deserted highway.

Then all of a sudden she was surrounded by lights. She recognized Lew's house. There had been a power failure in the area, she realized. Now lights were flickering on all across the countryside.

She dragged herself up the driveway to the porch of the house. Here she would stay until the rain eased again and she could go to her trailer.

A light flashed in her eyes.

"Marisa?" Lew's voice seemed to be coming from a long way off. "What the hell are you doing out here?"

"I'm—I'm—" Her breath was coming in convulsive disorder, "I think—"

"Hey, sweetheart," she heard him murmur as she was caught in his strong arms.

She felt herself being carried into the house until the pounding of the rain was on the roof above her head and not mercilessly against her skin.

He let her down on her unsteady feet. "Okay?" he asked.

She smiled wanly, realizing that she must look a sight. Lew's clothes were also wet and clinging to his body.

"I think you should take a hot bath," he told her. "We'll have explanations later. Go up and get dried off."

She hesitated, but then, feeling her hair dripping down her face and the soggy sandals on her feet, she moved toward the stairs.

Lew followed her.

"Where are you going?" she asked him.

"To dry off," he told her.

"But—" She slowed down on the stairs. His khaki cotton pants and shirt clung to the contours of his body. Marisa wondered if her clothes were as revealing.

"Look, sweetheart," he said, holding on to her arm and propeling her up the stairs, "I'm not intending on catching pneumonia just because you are caught in a fit of modesty. After all, we are married aren't we? I mean I've seen it all before."

"Let me go," she screamed.

"Now, now," he said calmly. "Are we going to act like human beings or animals?"

He walked over to a door and pushed it inward.

"You know where everything is," he said. "I'm sorry it's all I have to offer, but the other rooms are still being repaired."

She walked meekly toward the bedroom and entered.

"You can use the bathroom first," he told her. "There are plenty of towels and you can wear the robe hanging inside the door."

"What about you?"

"Do you care?" he said. "I'll change out here. Now get in there, Marisa, before you catch cold."

She went into the bathroom and closed the door behind her, deciding not to turn the massive old-fashioned key. At least she could trust Lew that much!

She peeled off the wet clothes and put on the navy robe that was hanging behind the door. It was much too big for her, so she pulled the cord around her twice to keep it from gaping open. She towel-dried her hair and hung her clothes over the towel-rack. She could see rain pounding against the window pane amid flashes of lightning and cracks of thunder.

There was a rap on the door.

"May I come in?" Lew asked.

She opened the door. He was standing by the door dressed in only a pair of dry jeans.

"I need a towel," he said, "before you have your bath."

"I'm not having a bath," she told him. "There's no need."

"Of course there's a need. I'm not asking why you were out there floundering around in the dark and wet. I presume you've got a car stuck up there somewhere on the highway. You must have walked quite a way and may well catch a chill."

He went to the bathtub and turned on the taps. Steaming water pounded out.

"Now, do as I say." He left her, after taking a towel from the rack for himself. He closed the door behind him.

Marisa turned the key.

Chapter Fourteen

He was right, Marisa thought as she sank into the glorious warm water. A hot bath did wonders for a wet shivery skin. She soaked for a long time, until the water cooled, then she stepped out onto the soft fluffy mat and rubbed herself dry with a huge towel. One thing about Lew, he enjoyed all the luxuries. Unless all these extras were for the women in his life. She could not help wondering.

She put the terry robe on again. Her hair was now beginning to dry in soft tendrils around her face. There was no one in the bedroom. Barefoot, she went out on the landing and down toward the kitchen. She could hear Lew moving about.

"Hi," he said casually. He was heating cocoa in a pan on the stove. "Some rain storm! I haven't seen one like this for years!"

Lightning flashed through the room, followed by the ominous rumbling of thunder.

"Scared of storms?" he asked.

"Just the thunder," she told him and sat down at the kitchen table.

His hair had dried in rough curls. He'd put on a navy sweatshirt over the jeans, but was still barefoot.

He brought the pan of cocoa to the table and poured it into the mugs. "Okay, what happened?" he asked.

"My car just stopped," she explained. "Out there somewhere." She waved her arm.

"Why didn't you wait until morning to come back?"

"It wasn't raining when I left."

"So you walked?"

She nodded.

"Why didn't you just sit there and wait until the rain subsided?"

"I only just managed to push the car off to the side of the road," Marisa told him slightly impatiently. "Something might have come along and hit me."

"Well that's true." he agreed, taking a sip of the hot chocolate.

"I'm sorry I've caused you a lot of bother."

"No bother," he said. "No bother at all, actually. It's rather nice to have company."

"Alicia not here?" she remarked.

"Now, let's not get catty," he told her. "Drink your chocolate like a good girl."

"Sounds like the storm's over," Lew said. He pulled back the checkered drapes. Sure enough, the rain had stopped, and the moon was forcing its way out of the clouds.

"I guess I should get to my trailer then." Marisa stood up. She really didn't want to leave the warm kitchen. She felt so at home, wearing Lew's robe and drinking hot chocolate in the comfortable farmhouse kitchen. She stifled a sigh.

"Whatever you want," he said coldly.

Marisa got up and left the kitchen, murmuring about seeing if her clothes were dry.

She went into Lew's bedroom and through to the bathroom. Her jeans were still heavy and wet, although her blouse was dry.

"Not dry?" Lew asked from the doorway. He must have followed her upstairs.

Marisa looked down at the robe. "I could go across in this," she said.

"If I care to lend it, yes," he told her.

"Will you?"

"No." He shook his head, his eyes alive with amusement. "I won't lend you anything."

"Then I'll wear the jeans," she said angrily, taking off the robe forgetting for a minute that he was there. The robe dropped to the floor. She had on only a bra and panties. She grabbed at the robe again to cover herself.

"Stop leering at me!" she shouted at him.

"I've seen it all before, as I told you," he said. "But it's quite nice to see it again. Pleasant, isn't that your word?"

"Lew, please," she appealed to him, holding the robe with trembling fingers.

Then before she could stop him, he'd flicked the robe from her hands. It tumbled to the floor.

"Lew—"

"Come on," he said, his breath fanning her face. His hands spanned her waist as he drew her through the door back into the bedroom. "You want me as much as I want you. Why don't we do something about it?"

"Because I'm not that type."

"You're my wife!"

"Not for three years." Her blue eyes filled with tears. "Oh please stop."

"I haven't started yet," he muttered. He leaned forward and took possession of her lips. She had no further desire to fight him. Soon she was running her fingers through his hair and up beneath his sweatshirt. He removed her lacy bra. Her breasts were trapped against the roughness of his chest.

"Lew" she murmured, when his lips left hers for one empty moment. She drew his head toward her again, to once more capture his mouth.

"Stay with me tonight." His voice was harsh with emotion.

"Yes, oh yes," she whispered.

Marisa opened her eyes and gazed out the window. Sunshine was streaming through the beige and brown curtains. For a moment, she couldn't think where she was. Then it all came back to her—the wanton desire that Lew had aroused in her, and then satisfied.

She rolled over in the bed toward the tanned, turned back. She still loved Lew. That had been obvious last night. Whatever she might have pretended, she still loved him. And Lew? Did he want to resume their relationship as husband and wife? Could she ever trust him? Trust was necessary in marriage, especially in their professions when they were repeatedly separated, and meeting new and glamorous people. She turned on her back and Lew turned to her, stretching his body and smiling sleepily from half-closed eyes.

"Morning," he murmured.

"Morning," she said. It was one thing to have him make love to her in the darkness. Another to wake up beside him in bright daylight.

He hooked one naked leg across hers, then leaned over and kissed her persuasively. "You're even more beautiful after a night's sleep," he said, his voice husky with sleep.

"What's the time?" she asked, her voice trembling.

"Damn the time." He kissed her again. She found herself being swept away once more into the vortex of his lovemaking.

When she awoke a second time, it was to the sound of running water in the bathroom. Lew came out of the bathroom in his underwear, "Hi. I thought I'd drive down the road and see about your car."

"Fine," she said, pulling the sheet up around her neck, suddenly aware of her nakedness.

"It's a great day today. Lots of sunshine." He went to the closet and took out a pair of denim pants and a navy shirt.

"Are my clothes dry?" Marisa asked.

"I think so." He went back into the bathroom, buttoning his shirt. He came out with her jeans and top and windbreaker. "All in one piece," he said, slipping them onto a chair. He leaned over and kissed her, "I'll be back shortly. We'll have breakfast eh?"

She nodded, and after another brief kiss, he left her. She heard him go down the stairs and out the front door. His car started up and crunched over the gravel driveway.

Chapter Fifteen

Marisa got up slowly. The air felt warm inside the house, promising another hot day.

She dressed in her jeans and top, now dry. So Lew wanted breakfast, well, so did she. She went downstairs to the kitchen. She had to pass the study. It looked as though Lew had left his work in a rush. There was paper strewn around, piled in crumpled heaps near his desk. She wandered over to the typewriter where there was a sheet of paper almost completely typed.

After reading the narrative she realized that this wasn't a play or a script, but a novel. Lew had really meant what he'd said. He was writing a book. She wondered if he intended to go on living in this house. It was a perfect place to complete a novel. Peaceful and isolated, not like the house he owned in California. This was a family house. A place where you'd want to raise children and dogs. But not with her. He had never discussed it with her. Could it be Alicia?

The thought stabbed her. She left the study abruptly, moving toward the kitchen. She would cook breakfast and then get back to her trailer. Last night had been madness, brought on by the storm and the intimacy of being trapped together in the house. Nothing more. She couldn't expect love. Had he ever said he'd loved her? Marisa could never really think of a time. Desired her, wanted her, but never loved her.

She sighed and moved around the kitchen, checking the cupboards. They were well-stocked with cans of food as if he expected a long hard winter here. The fridge was full too. Plenty of eggs, bacon, sausages.

The front door slammed, just as she cracked the eggs into the pan.

"Now, that smells good." Lew came into the kitchen and walked to the sink, turning on the taps to wash the grease and dirt from his hands. "I couldn't get your car started," he said. "It was soaking wet, but a couple of guys who own a garage in Parkville are going out to tow it in and fix it for you. I brought your luggage along though. It's in the hallway."

"I could have done all that," she said.

"No trouble," he murmured, giving her a warm smile.

They ate breakfast in silence, both so hungry that Marisa had to make extra toast. While waiting for it to pop up from the toaster, Lew said, "What do you want to do today?"

"You don't have to amuse me."

"I thought I should."

"Just because you—you—" she began.

"Took you to bed," he said. "No, not because of that."

The toast popped up and Marisa buttered it. She gave one of the slices to Lew.

He covered it with strawberry jam.

"Don't you have to work?" she said.

"I give myself a day off once in a while," he told her. "Why? Have you been nosing around in my study?"

"I wasn't nosing around. I just noticed that you were writing."

"I told you I was writing a book. I'm sick to death of commuting all over the world." He sighed and rubbed his hand against his chest inside his denim shirt.

"Then you're going to live here?" she asked.

He nodded, "I thought that might be obvious."

"Alone?" she said, so softly that she didn't think he'd hear her, but he did.

"That all depends," he told her, picking up his coffee and gulping it down.

"On what?" she asked tremulously.

He shook his head. "On lots of things." He stood up. "I thought I might take you over the property. There's a big barn in the back, no animals or horses, I'm sorry to say, but maybe I can remedy that soon."

"I'd like that," she said, realizing that she wanted to spend the rest of the day with him. The rest of the day, the rest of her life. She had to cling to small pleasures. Soon they would be divorced. Alicia would live here in this house with him, sharing his bed, his kitchen, his life. . . .

"I didn't realize that all this was yours," Marisa told Lew, spreading her arms around in the warm sunshine. "It stretches for miles."

They'd just come out of the barn. The fields extended before them, patched green and sunburned brown.

Marisa settled on the grass, drawing her legs up to her chin. "I grew up in the country," she said, "not far from here."

Lew sat down beside her, his denim clad thigh brushing against her own.

"What happened to your parents?" he asked.

"They were killed in a car crash. Then I lived with my aunt until she died."

"And then you went to California?" he asked.

She nodded. "And what about you?"

"I lived here," he told her. "Right on this piece of land. Unfortunately, my father sold the place when he retired to Florida, and I had to wait until now to buy it back."

"You have parents?" She had somehow always thought of him as a loner. A man without family ties. But there was this house and land, a family history.

"Of course I have parents, and a brother and sister. Neil lives in South America, hence the South American business connection and Patricia lives out in Vancouver. Neither had the money to buy the house when it went up for sale."

"Why didn't you buy it?" she asked.

He sighed, "I was away somewhere making a film.

My parents didn't know where to get hold of me. Dad's heart wasn't too good and it was all too much for him. I know he wanted to leave it to his children."

"You never told me any of this," she said.

"Did you ever ask?" He gave her a sideways glance. She shook her head.

"I'll admit it was as much my fault as yours," Lew told her. "I mean we didn't get much time alone. When we were home, there were always people there."

Marisa shifted restlessly on the prickly, brown grass. As she moved, their thighs touched. She hugged her knees closer to her. Even the smallest physical contact with Lew seemed to arouse her desire for him.

"What are you thinking?" Lew's voice broke into her thoughts.

"Just that it's a beautiful day," she lied, and rose abruptly. Any more time spent by his side and she would surely be begging him to make love again. She walked down the hill that led toward the house.

Lew joined her. "Shall we have dinner in town?" he asked.

"I don't think so Lew," she said, thoughtfully.

"Why not? I don't know about you, but eating alone is almost as bad as sleeping alone."

"Then that's why you've been doing your darndest to get plenty of company while you're out here," she told him.

He sighed, and took hold of her arm. "Why don't you quit baiting me Marisa? Just for today, can't we be friends?"

He stood in front of her, massive as a brick wall, unmovable. "Well?" he said.

"I think I'll get changed," she told him, and turned and walked toward her trailer.

"Half an hour?" he called after her.

She swung around and met his eyes. "Half an hour," she agreed.

Marisa took a shower. Then she chose a full skirted colorful print dress to wear. She brushed her hair. It looked almost silvery against her tanned skin.

Lew was as good as his word. In half an hour he knocked on her trailer door. He had changed into khaki pants and a matching shirt.

His eyes were approving as he looked her over.

"Ready?"

"Yes," she nodded. "Are you?"

"As ready as I'll ever be," he told her.

They dined in the Parkville Hotel, in a smaller room than the one in which the party had been held.

Lew made a conscious decision to stay away from anything too personal. They discussed the progress of the film. He was pleased that they were nearly ready to wind up shooting.

After lingering over coffee, they left the restaurant and drove back to the house.

When they got out of the car and were standing outside the house, Lew took her hand.

"Are you joining me again tonight?" he asked, looking at her intently in the half light of the sunset.

"I don't think so," she said. After all, it would soon be Alicia's house.

"Oh?" He raised an eyebrow. "Your values have changed. I didn't know you were into one-night stands."

"It was all a mistake," she murmured.

"Some mistake." Lew shoved his hands into the back pockets of his pants. "You realize you could get pregnant making a mistake like that."

"If it happens, it happens," she told him, wondering how she'd feel if she were carrying his child.

He turned abruptly to face her. "I can't quite understand what you're getting at, sweetheart. Last night you didn't give me the impression that you wanted a divorce."

She wiped her hand across her forehead. Didn't he realize that she couldn't live with him again? Not without trusting him. Would Alicia just take the place of Carla?

"I suppose there's someone else then?" he asked bleakly.

She shook her head, but he didn't believe her.

"Probably Benton," he went on. "I saw the way he looked at you at the studio that day. The way he's protected you all this time. You don't do that for a mere acquaintance."

"It's not—"

But Lew put up a warning hand. "Let's not hear anymore. I'll get on to that divorce as planned. Life's full of little surprises though. I guess last night was just one of them."

He smiled pleasantly. "It's been a nice day Marisa. Now, why don't you get to your trailer? We both have a lot of work to do this week."

"Lew—" She wanted to say all sorts of things to him, but she didn't know where to start. To have him look at her with that cool gray stare after the warmth of last night was almost unbearable.

"Don't, Marisa, we've said enough. I'll see you tomorrow." Then he turned away from her and walked quickly toward the house. He opened the door, walked in, and closed it immediately behind him.

Chapter Sixteen

The following week didn't go well. It was now September. The weather became cooler with rain. Production halted. This meant they would have to go over schedule into late September, which made everyone irritable.

Lew was cool and tightly coiled as a spring. Marisa cowered beneath his icy glances. Alicia Allen seemed to be the only person to coax an occasional smile from him.

They weren't doing the easiest part of the film either. It was the last part. Marion's marriage to Roland just a few days before her suicide. Marisa could not keep her mind on the passionate love scenes she had to act with Paul. The thought that she loved Lew Stone even after their painful parting was devastating to her.

"Marisa!" Lew yelled at her one day when she seemed so out of step that she wondered if she would ever do anything right again. "Show some warmth, woman. This is the man you love. The man you're prepared to kill yourself over. Respond to him, baby, please."

Finally she managed to please him. At last they finished the filming.

There was a farewell party. It was going to be held on the patio at the back of the house. Some of the crew were stringing up lights and adding spotlights. They had set up a stereo and speakers for dancing. It was the end of their time together out here. As always, the occasion would be rather nostalgic. They had all worked hard together and become friends. Now they might never see each other again.

Marisa didn't really feel in the mood for a party, but she knew that she had to attend. She was part of the glamour, the star of the movie. She supposed she could have said yes to Lew's idea of a reconciliation. Just take up where they'd left off three years ago. No questions asked. No mention of love. Just the lust he'd always felt for her.

She wanted more than that. What happened when they were old and passion died? What then and what if there were children? Children needed, not a relationship built on lust and mistrust.

She sighed and looked at her reflection in the mirror. She'd chosen to wear a pair of blue string, a darker blue sweater. Her hair was a mass of curls. Her face was tanned and healthy, belying the sadness in her blue eyes. After a final spray of perfume, she left her trailer to join the others gathering on the patio.

Here dancing was inte with a barbecue

continuously issuing hot dogs, hamburgers and steaks. A grand array of salads was spread out on a table. Lew made sure that everyone had a full glass in hand. Marisa noticed that he was circulating easily, dancing with all the women. He was wearing a pair of navy cords with a navy sweater. Marisa thought wistfully that she had never seen him look more handsome and attractive.

Paul Dexter also looked attractive, although he seemed a little unsteady on his feet, Marisa thought, as he walked toward her to claim his dance.

"Haven't you eaten anything Paul?" she asked, recoiling slightly from his alcoholic breath.

"I don't eat while I'm drinking," he said. "Come on, beautiful, let's dance."

Marisa slipped into his arms, and they danced across the patio to a slow waltz. He held her tightly, his fingers moving up and down her spine. When the dance was over he said, "Let's go for a walk."

Marisa agreed, and they moved away from the smell of coal-broiled food and loud music.

"it's over," Marisa said brightly. "Do you think we did good job?"

"even" Paul slurred. Marisa realized that he was even drunk than she'd thought.

Maybe they should go into the house and she'd make him a coffee. She pushed open the door, Paul following ly. They went to the kitchen.

"Hey re you doing?" he asked, shading his eyes as turned on the light.

"Makoffee to sober you up," she told him.

"Honeffee to sober you up," she told him. He came and slung his arm across her shoule on her heavily.

"You're drunk Paul," she told him, trying to push him away.

But he was too strong for her. Before she knew it, she was being pushed up against the wall, and he was planting hot kisses against her throat and neck.

"Paul—" She struggled against him. "Paul, please, this is stupid. You're drunk."

"Not too drunk to make love to you, Marisa," he mumbled. "Come on sweetheart." He looked into her face, "You don't say no to Lew Stone, why do you say no to me?"

"I don't know what you're talking about," she said coldly.

"Oh yes you do," Paul told her. "You know very well."

"No please—" She shook her head as he planted more kisses down the side of her neck. "Please let me go."

Then she heard the ringing of the telephone coming from the study.

"The phone," she said unnecessarily. Paul seemed to be distracted by the noise. She escaped from his grasp. Running into the study, she picked up the phone.

"Hello," she said breathlessly.

"Is Lew Stone there?" a silky, female voice asked.

"He's outside," Marisa told her. "I'll see if I can locate him."

"It's very urgent," the female voice said. It seemed as though she had been crying. Was she another of Lew's loves?

"I'll see what I can do," Marisa promised the girl. "Just hold on."

Out on the patio Lew was dancing with Alicia. She'd

have to interrupt that love scene. Another one of his women needed him.

She went over to them and tapped Lew's arm.

"Lew," she said tentatively.

"What is it, Marisa?" He loosened his hold on Alicia.

"There's a phone call for you in the study. A woman," she added. It was fun to see a spark of jealousy light up Alicia's eyes.

"I'll take it," Lew said. Marisa watched with satisfaction as he strode off into the house.

"You think you can give him orders," Alicia said, "just because you're his ex-wife."

"At least I have the privilege of being his ex-wife, not just a passing fancy," Marisa said smugly. "Let's make it clear," she went on, "we're not divorced yet."

Just give it time," Alicia said. "Lew wants to be rid of you."

"I don't doubt it," Marisa said sounding more sure of herself than she was. She added sweetly, "Shouldn't we leave it up to him?"

"Maybe I should go and see who that was on the phone," Alicia said, obviously ill at ease.

They came across Lew standing in the hallway. He was staring into space and for a moment he didn't notice them. Marisa saw the pain in his eyes and the pinched look of his face. She touched his arm.

"Lew?" she whispered, forgetting that Alicia was watching her. "What is it?"

"My father's dead," he said. He brushed her aside and headed out the front door, slamming it behind him.

Chapter Seventeen

Marisa went upstairs to Lew's bedroom. She'd packed for Lew's trips before and knew that he always took the worn leather case for short trips. She pulled it out of his closet and opened a drawer in the dresser. She began packing for him. Then she heard the front door slam and slow, heavy footsteps on the stairs. Suddenly, Lew was standing at the bedroom door.

She licked dry lips, "I'm sorry," she said inadequately.

"It almost sounds like you mean that," he said.

"I do. I got some things ready for you."

"The sweet little wife," he said. "Thanks."

"Do you want me to book you a flight?"

"Miami," he told her. "If you don't mind?"

"No." She shook her head. "Anything else?"

"No," he sighed. "I'd like to be left alone, if you don't mind?"

"Of course."

In the study she booked him on the morning flight to Miami. She had to tell him his flight information so she went up to his room. He was still dressed, lying down on the bed, his head propped against a pillow.

"Lew," she said quietly.

"Yes," he glanced at her.

"I wrote down your flight on the pad by the phone. It leaves in the morning."

"Thanks," he said, and then, "Come here, Marisa."

She went and stood beside the bed.

"We probably won't see each other again," he said. "I want to thank you for doing 'The Rain Lady.' I hope it's a success."

"It will be," she told him, realizing that the film had meant much more to him than just another job. Her heart ached for him.

"Also, Marisa, my lawyer will probably be contacting you about the divorce. I think it should be pretty smooth sailing."

A lump formed in her throat. She nodded.

"If you want to see the rushes, Benton'll see to that. I know you usually don't."

She shook her head. Tears formed in her eyes and were now running freely down her face. Lew reached up and wiped them away with his fingers.

"Are you crying for me?" he asked. She nodded. "Thanks," he said. "It's been a long time since anyone cried for me."

Then he pulled her towards him and kissed her. His kiss was warm and tender.

"Take care, honey," he said. Marisa was too choked up to say good-bye. She ran from the room.

Lew left early in the morning before anyone else was up.

Marisa had packed halfheartedly and was rounding up her toiletry articles when Paul Dexter poked his head around the corner of her trailer door.

He looked rather the worse for wear. His eyes were red and bloodshot, his skin yellow.

"I'm sorry about last night Marisa," he said.

"Forget it," Marisa said briefly.

"Alicia told me that Stone was your husband."

"More or less," Marisa told him.

Paul smiled, "Well, anyhow I'm sorry. In case we have to work together again, I don't want this to affect our working relationship."

"Please, Paul, I have some packing to do."

"Sure. See you."

Marisa continued packing, smiling to herself. She wouldn't be fooled by Paul. He would still spread gossip, however sincere he sounded. She snapped the fastener on her suitcase with a click.

There was a knock on her door. It was Jean.

"Everything okay?" Jean asked.

"Fine," Marisa told her. "I'll be leaving shortly. Will I see you again?"

"If you're ever down in L.A.," Jean told her. "It was hard luck about Lew's dad."

"Yes it was," Marisa said.

"I've known Lew for a long time," Jean went on. "He's a great person."

"I'm sure he must be," Marisa murmured.

"Well I have to go. It was nice working with you. Good luck and good-bye."

"Good-bye Jean," Marisa said.

Before getting into her car, Marisa walked around the house. She'd like to stay here in this house with Lew and never leave. But that wasn't possible. He had his work, she had hers, and he had Alicia Allen.

Marisa got into her red sports car, started the engine, and drove off. Lew Stone was now out of her life, but would he ever be out of her heart?

Chapter Eighteen

There was a pile of mail waiting for her at her apartment and a message from John on her answering service to call him immediately. She put the mail aside and dialed John's phone number.

"You called?" Marisa said when he answered.

"Marisa? Yes. How are you, sweetheart?"

"Tired," she said. "How are you?"

"Absolutely delirious. I'm back with Clara and the kids. Everything's fine."

"I'm glad John," she told him.

"I have a couple of film offers for you. Interested?"

"I suppose I should be," she told him. How could she explain that this encounter with Lew had drained her of all energy?

"Okay, honey. You want a rest is that it?"

"Maybe just a few days," she told him. "Then I'll come in and see you."

"Fine. There's a bit of time," John told her. "Did everything wind up successfully up there?"

"I think we did a good job," Marisa said.

"Good. Lew Stone seemed pleased when I talked to him yesterday. See you then, sweetheart."

"Bye, John," she said, and hung up the phone.

She took her luggage to her bedroom. She'd unpack later. Sitting on the side of her bed, wearily running her hand through her hair, she caught her reflection in the mirror. The dark shadows beneath her eyes made her face look thinner than usual and her full mouth was sad. The tears that she had been holding back for weeks now, streamed down her cheeks unchecked.

John had two film offers for her, one in Toronto, one out in California. She chose the one in Toronto. California held too many memories of Lew.

She wondered where he was. Back in L.A. recovering from his father's death or up north in his house in Parkville writing his novel? Was Alicia Allen with him, comforting him? The thought burned and burrowed deep in the crevices of her soul.

She wasn't to start work until January, so she had all December and Christmas to occupy herself before that time. She'd visited with John and Clara. Clara had kindly invited her to spend Christmas with them. She probably would if she could stand to see the happiness radiating from all of the Bentons' faces.

It was a snowy winter day and she'd been downtown to buy Christmas gifts for John's children. She parked her car downstairs in the underground garage and took the elevator to her floor.

The effort of fighting the crowds had left her rather

weak. She hadn't been eating very well the last weeks and there was a gaunt look to her face and body that made her look pale and fragile. She hadn't been sleeping either. She was relying on a supply of sleeping pills, but that supply was slowly dwindling. It scared her to think she was right back where she'd pulled herself up from a couple of years ago.

A man was pacing the thickly carpeted corridor outside her apartment door. She thought there was something vaguely familiar about him.

She was about to insert the key in the lock of her door when he approached her.

"Marisa?" he asked. She turned to look at him, immediately recognizing the plump, tanned features.

"Mark?"

He held out his hand. "Mark Lawson, remember me?"

"Of course. How are you?"

"Not bad," he said. "I'd like to talk to you if I may."

"Of course." Marisa shuffled her parcels, and pushed open her front door. "Why don't you come in?"

"Would you like some coffee?" she asked. His features were pinched by cold.

"Please," Mark said. "This weather is terrible."

"A bit of a change from California I'll admit," Marisa said. "When did you get in?"

"A couple of hours ago."

"Did you come straight here?" she asked.

He nodded, "I had to see you."

Was it about Lew? *The divorce?* She didn't want to know, quite yet. "I'll get the coffee. Why don't you sit down."

When Marisa came out of the kitchen, Mark was

sitting down rubbing his hands together as though he were still cold.

"I'm sorry I haven't got a roaring fire," she told him. "I'll turn the heat up if you like."

"No, it's fine." Mark smiled. "It's just the abrupt change in temperature.

Placing the tray on the coffee table, Marisa sat down beside him on the sofa. "How are Barbara and the kids?" she asked.

"They're all fine. We have another boy now. Born last year," Mark said. He rubbed his hands together again.

Marisa realized suddenly that he was nervous, not cold.

"What did you come here for?" she asked, afraid to hear his answer.

He pushed at his sun-bleached brown hair, "It's about Lew," he said.

"What about him?" she asked, sharply taking in a breath.

"Nothing really. I hope," Mark said. "He was supposed to have arrived in L.A. on a flight last weekend. He didn't show up."

"Have you checked the airport. Did he cancel?" Marisa felt her heartbeat quicken.

"I checked. I also checked all the hospitals."

"Hospitals?" Marisa paled. If anything had happened to Lew—anything at all, she'd . . .

"Apparently he went to the airport and was about to board the plane when he collapsed. He was taken to the hospital where he discharged himself."

"Why did he collapse?" Marisa asked.

"Apparently he was in a state of complete exhaustion. That's all I could get out of them. Would you have any idea where he might be?" Mark asked.

"Up at his house. That's the only place I can think of. I have his number if you want to phone."

"I think I should."

Marisa gave Mark Lew's phone number and went into the bedroom. She didn't want to hear the conversation between the two men. So it hadn't been her imagination when she'd noticed the lines of strain and tension in Lew's face.

There was a knock at the bedroom door.

"He's there," Mark told her. "It's nothing to worry about. Too much work and his father's death hit him hard."

"I'm glad you found him," Marisa said, forcing a smile, realizing that she was trembling. It had been a shock to see Mark Lawson, another shock to know that Lew was ill.

Mark sat down on the couch again and helped himself to more coffee, relaxed now that he knew where Lew was and that he was safe.

"He's writing a novel. Did you know that?" Mark said cheerfully. "It should be a smashing best seller."

"I'm sure it will be," Marisa said with conviction. She had never doubted Lew's abilities.

"I'm surprised you're not up there living with him now! Are you making another film down here?" Mark asked innocently.

"Why should I be living with him?" Marisa asked.

"Because he finally found you. I mean that was his intention apart from 'The Rain Lady.'"

"His intention?" Marisa repeated Mark's words. "What do you mean his intention?"

"He got that house, so he could stop flying back and forth around the world and settle down to writing books, being with you and maybe having children."

"Lew wanted that?" she said, her voice just a whisper. Mark was joking, surely he was joking.

"Lew wanted a divorce," she told him. "Didn't he tell you that? He'd contacted his lawyer in L.A."

"Barrett?" Mark asked in surprise.

"Whoever his lawyer is," Marisa said.

"He never contacted Barrett, nor said a word to me."

"But that weekend he went back?" Marisa prodded, "Didn't he tell you then?"

"No. He was elated, he'd found you."

"But he doesn't love me," Marisa told Mark. "He's never loved me."

"I think he does love you Marisa," Mark said. "He was devastated when you left him. It was almost as if he were a different person, but he managed to gain some kind of control and threw himself into his work. For months no one knew where he was or what he was doing. In the end he produced 'The Rain Lady' script. Then he set about looking for you to play the part of Marion. When he finally found you, he had to break through with John Benton. Well, you know the rest. He should have told you this himself. With Lew, it's his pride. Or maybe you haven't given him any indication that you want him back. I don't know—"

Marisa shook her head, feeling as though she were dreaming.

Mark went on. "He was hurt once before by an actress on the rise. He vowed never to be hurt again, but when he met you—"

"Who?" Marisa interrupted.

"Carla Tomlin," Mark said, "she was a nasty little gold-digger. Took him for all she could get. Then, when he became successful, she started latching on to him again."

"But he still wanted her."

"He admired her talent. In the end, that was all."

Marisa remembered the newspaper article: "Miss Tomlin says it's love." Not *Lew Stone*, but *Miss Tomlin*. Had she pre-judged him without knowing the facts?

"Maybe I should go to him, Mark," she said softly. "Do you think so?"

"He sounded very down," Mark told her. "It might be a good idea. If you still love him, that is."

"Of course, I love him." Marisa felt a lump rise in her throat, "I've always loved him."

"Then go and see him. Talk to him. You may have to break down his pride." He smiled reminiscently. "I know how you feel. Lew and I have had our differences too."

Marisa smiled back. "Thank you for coming Mark. I am really grateful to you. You are a good friend to both of us." She stretched out her hand to Mark who pressed it gently before releasing it. Their eyes met with understanding.

The roads up north were icy. Fresh snow was falling covering the ice and Marisa was terrified of skidding. She noticed that there had been several accidents along the way. Though the driving required her hard concentration, she could not help thinking about what Mark had told her. *Lew loved her and was devastated when she'd left him.* But why hadn't he ever told her of his feelings?

The car slid on the icy road and she turned her thoughts completely to her driving. She wasn't going to get stranded tonight. Tonight, she had to arrive in one piece and in full command of her senses.

It was slow going, even slight pressure on the accelerator caused the car to skid wildly. She proceeded slowly and cautiously. She must *get to Lew*.

What if Mark was wrong though? What if Lew didn't really love her? What if he really did want a divorce because now Alicia Allen had come along to fill the gap Marisa had left? Mark didn't know about Alicia, did he? She tried to suppress these negative thoughts and concentrate on the difficult driving.

Finally, she arrived at her destination. She turned off the road to drive up to the house. It had not been cleared. She parked the car by the side of the road and got out, dragging her purse and small overnight bag with her. It was very cold. Marisa could feel the biting wind right through her sheepskin coat. She began to walk, stumbling as she made her way through the deep, wet snow.

"You made it." Lew's rasping voice startled her in the darkness. She could dimly make out the outline of his large figure looming toward her.

"Yes," she said breathlessly.

"Mark phoned. If I could have stopped you coming, I would have."

"I would have come anyway," she said. She followed him up onto the porch and through the lighted doorway into the warmth of the front foyer. Pushing back her hood, she wiped the snow from her face. Then she looked up at Lew.

He was wearing an old navy blue parka. He took

down the hood and she saw his unshaven face with a few days growth of beard.

"I don't know why the hell you drove all this way in a snowstorm," he told her, his eyes masklike and cold. His breath, she noticed, reeked of alcohol.

"Didn't Mark tell you?" she asked, taking off her coat, and straightening her sweater beneath it.

"Mark just said you were on your way. What nonsense did you two plot?"

"Oh Lew," she sighed, realizing that he was in no mood to be reasonable. Maybe they should wait until morning before talking. She could sleep on the couch downstairs.

He walked over and slammed the front door where the snow was blowing in. Then he took off his parka and hung it deliberately in the front hall closet.

"What the hell am I supposed to do now that you're here?" he asked, turning to face her.

"What do you usually do with a wife?" She held her ground.

He stared at her without answering.

The place was dusty and unkempt. Looking through to the study, Marisa could see that it was in a state of chaos. An empty whiskey bottle stood beside the typewriter. "How long have you been like this?" she asked.

"Like what?" He was wearing a thick black sweater and a pair of crumpled jeans. His hair was disheveled, his eyes were cadaverous in his pale face.

"Like this—half drunk. Collapsing at airports."

"Do you care?"

"What if I said I did?" she confronted him bravely.

"Then I'd say you were lying." he told her, and lurched toward her. "Now get lost, I'm working."

"I can't leave now."

"I know that. But there are lots of rooms. We don't have to get under each other's feet."

"Are you alone here?" she asked.

"No I've got a harem up in the bedroom," he sneered. "Care to check?"

"Okay," she said, "so you're alone."

She put her purse down on a chair in the corner, "Would you like me to fix some coffee?"

"You can do what you want," he said, striding toward the study. He closed the door in her face.

Marisa went into the kitchen. It was a mess—empty whiskey bottles and a sink full of dishes. Lew must have been trying to drink himself to death, Marisa thought, as she pushed the bottles into the garbage can. Then she rolled up her sleeves and set about to clean the kitchen.

It took a while but eventually, she had the kitchen almost spotless. She heated a can of soup and made corned beef sandwiches and coffee from Lew's meager supplies. When the meal was ready, she knocked on the study door. When there was no answer, she pushed open the door and entered.

Lew was standing at the window looking out at the snow flakes whirling toward the ground.

"Lew?" she said timidly. "I've made some soup and sandwiches. You could probably do with a meal."

He turned slowly, his hands thrust deeply into the back pockets of his jeans.

"You shouldn't have bothered," he said coldly. "I'm not denying myself food or liquid."

"I noticed the liquid," she told him, "but I want you to eat. I don't want to hear any more stories about you collapsing at airports."

"Mark's an idiot," he said, tottering.

"Mark was worried," she told him. "That was all. He came to me because I'm your wife. Now will you come and eat."

Surprisingly, he walked to the door and followed her meekly into the kitchen. Marisa served the strong coffee, soup and sandwiches. They ate in silence, finishing all the food.

Marisa watched Lew. She knew that she herself looked thin and undernourished with dark shadows beneath her eyes from lack of sleep, but Lew looked even worse. She noticed that when he placed his empty coffee mug back on the table, he was almost asleep.

"Why don't you go up to bed?" she suggested. "I'll clean up."

He got up and walked toward the kitchen door. She heard his footsteps move unsteadily on the stairs. No fight, no suggestions that she spend the night with him. Just a resigned meekness. Oh Lew she thought, her heart aching. She followed him upstairs. He'd already collapsed across the bed when she got there. She managed to get his shoes and socks off but left him in the jeans and sweater. Pulling the quilt over him as best she could, she turned off the light and closed the door.

Chapter Nineteen

When Marisa woke up, the sun was streaming in through the window. A lump from the Victorian sofa jabbed into her cold back. Her sheepskin coat had slipped onto the floor. She could smell coffee in the kitchen and hear the sizzle of bacon. She lay back, luxuriating, in spite of the lumpiness of her makeshift bed. But who was cooking? Lew?

There was a noise outside the door and Lew poked his head through. He'd shaved and showered and he was dressed in clean jeans and a sweater. Except for the heaviness of his eyes and tautness of his skin, he looked quite presentable.

"Sleeping beauty," he said, caustically, "are you hungry?"

"It smells delicious," she smiled. "Do you feel any better?"

"I'm still here, if that's any consolation," he told her. "It wasn't my intention."

"What do you mean?" She eased herself up on the sofa and swung her legs around.

"What do you think I mean?"

"Oh no," she looked at him aghast, "you wouldn't have."

"When there is nothing left to live for. . . ." he said.

"But you've got everything to live for." She stood up, straightening the slacks and sweater that she'd slept in. "You're rich, famous, talented—"

"So were you, and I hear that wasn't enough for you either," he told her.

"I—" She glanced around her. "That was foolishness, I was ill—"

He smiled cynically. "And I made you ill?"

"Yes," she said, wondering why she'd ever come all this distance to face this madman.

"And you made me ill? That's what Mark Lawson told you wasn't it?"

She nodded. "Lew," she said, "I came here to talk, not to quarrel. If anything had happened to you, I couldn't have stood it."

"What do you care?" he asked roughly. "You would have been rid of me for good. There wouldn't have had to be a divorce, just a funeral."

"Don't! Don't say those things! Mark told me all about how you felt when I left. About Carla—"

He sighed heavily, "So he's told you everything has he? How much I love you. How I can't live without you. How I searched for you and found you and how—" his voice grew husky. "And how you don't want me now that I've found you. Did you tell him that, my love?"

"It's not true," she whispered, shaken by his outburst.

"Why?" He eyed her cautiously, "Because now you've found out I still love you, you want to return to your rich husband is that it?"

"No," she said hoarsely. "That's not it."

"Then what is it?" His expression was stony.

"I want to return because I love you," she said.

He shook his head from side to side. "I don't believe you. If you'd loved me, you'd never have left in the first place. You'd have waited to hear my explanations, you would not have run off like a scared rabbit."

"Oh, Lew, tell me the truth now at last. Was Carla Tomlin your mistress?"

"No," he said. "Never. Not even before I met you when I thought I loved her."

Marisa's lips trembled. She couldn't speak.

He arched an eyebrow. "You've wasted your energy, my love, wondering about me in bed with other women when there's no one in the world I have ever wanted but you."

"You never told me you loved me," she whispered.

"Did I need to? I thought there was no question. We were together." His eyes softened. "I love you," he said simply. "I always have."

Light as a feather, she flew into his arms.

"Benton kept me away from you for a long time," he murmured huskily, after breaking from their first, long kiss. "Was there anything between you two?"

"No," she whispered. "He was just a good friend. He's gone back to his wife."

"I'm glad. I don't want any competition." He laughed shakily, "Did you tell him to keep you in hiding?"

She nodded, "I was ill for a long time. It's only this last year that I was strong enough to even consider working again."

He stroked her hair. "I'm sorry, darling. I should have explained about Carla, but just the thought that you didn't trust me, that you really believed that I would be unfaithful, infuriated me. That terrible evening I went to Mark's house, not to Carla, then, I had a business appointment I couldn't break and when I got home the next evening, you were gone. I searched for you through every agent. As you know, Benton kept your secret."

They kissed again. "One thing," Lew murmured against the softness of her skin, where he'd pushed her sweater aside, "would you mind living here in this house, raising children and forgetting about the outside world for a while?"

"As long as I'm with you," she told him breathlessly. "And this is my dream house."

"Buried in snow for half the winter?" He smiled down at her.

"Why not, with you?" she grinned mischievously, then pulled away from him and went to find her purse. She picked it up, opened it, and took out a small ring box. Inside was a gold wedding band. She held it out to her husband. "I'd like you to put this on me again," she told him softly.

"You mean you kept it?"

"Of course."

He took it from her, letting it lay in his tanned palm.

"Is there anything else that's bothering you? Anything else that could stand between us?" he asked, idly watching the gold band glint in the sunlight drifting through the window.

"No," she said, and then, "yes, there is something else."

"What?" He looked worried.

"Alicia Allen? Did you, was she—?"

He smiled gently, "No. I was using her to make you jealous. I didn't think I'd succeeded."

"You did, you know," she told him smiling.

"You hid everything wonderfully. You're an excellent actress." He pulled her close once more, taking her ring finger. "Okay this is it, my love, for better or for worse. Nothing will ever come between us again." He slipped the gold band on to Marisa's left hand, then bent down to kiss her fingers.

"One other thing," she said, when he raised his head.

"Now what?" he sighed.

"I thought you'd cooked me breakfast?"

"It will keep," he murmured, his mouth close to her smiling lips.

Silhouette Romance

ROMANCE THE WAY
IT USED TO BE...
AND COULD BE AGAIN

Contemporary romances for today's women

Each month, six very special love stories will be yours from SILHOUETTE. Look for them wherever books are sold or order now from the coupon below.

SILHOUETTE BOOKS, Department SB/1
1230 Avenue of the Americas, New York, N.Y. 10020

Please send me the books I have checked above. I am enclosing $_____
(please add 50¢ to cover postage and handling for each order, N.Y.S. and N.Y.C.
residents please add appropriate sales tax). Send check or money order—no
cash or C.O.Ds please. Allow up to six weeks for delivery.

NAME_____

ADDRESS_____

CITY_____ STATE/ZIP_____

SB/9/80